CONTENTS

KU-336-385

PUFFIN BOOKS
THE RIDDLING REAVER

In *Fighting Fantasy – The Introductory Role-playing Game*, an extra dimension was added to the Puffin Fighting Fantasy Game-books. The simple and fast-moving game system invented by Steve Jackson and Ian Livingstone allows you, as GamesMaster in a full-fledged role-playing game, to invent thrilling missions

Croft School
Stratford-upon-Avon

Dulce et Forte

Awarded to

Michael Toolan

for

Progress in Form 4

FIGHTING FANTASY GAMEBOOKS

Steve Jackson's *SORCERY!*

FIGHTING FANTASY – The Introductory Role-playing Game
OUT OF THE PIT – Fighting Fantasy Monsters
TITAN – The Fighting Fantasy World

Edited by
STEVE JACKSON

THE RIDDLING REAVER

Paul Mason and Steve Williams

Illustrated by
Brian Williams and Leo Hartas

Puffin Books

To Carolina and my feet (without whom I would have been unable to get up in the morning)

Puffin Books, Penguin Books Ltd, Harmondsworth, Middlesex, England
Viking Penguin Inc., 40 West 23rd Street, New York, New York 10010, U.S.A.
Penguin Books Australia Ltd, Ringwood, Victoria, Australia
Penguin Books Canada Limited, 2801 John Street, Markham, Ontario,
Canada L3R 1B4
Penguin Books (N.Z.) Ltd, 182–190 Wairau Road, Auckland 10, New Zealand

First published 1986
Reprinted 1987

Made and printed in Great Britain by
Cox & Wyman Ltd, Reading
Filmset in Linotron Palatino by
Rowland Phototypesetting Ltd,
Bury St Edmunds, Suffolk

INTRODUCTION

Welcome to the world of Fighting Fantasy role-playing!

You and your friends are about to embark on an epic quest, one that will take you from the splendour of Kallamehr, across the treacherous Gulf of Shamuz, and into the sweaty southern jungles of Allansia. Throughout your quest, you will be chased, taunted, led astray, bedevilled and generally harassed by the most unpredictable of enemies – the Riddling Reaver.

This game works well with three players (and one GamesMaster), better with four players, and best with five players, which is probably also the maximum number desirable.

In order to use this book, you must have *Fighting Fantasy – The Introductory Role-playing Game* by Steve Jackson, which contains a full explanation of the rules of the game, and details of equipment and so on that players have. If you are the GamesMaster, then you should make sure that you are familiar with the *Fighting Fantasy* system before starting to run the game. You will also find it very useful to have *Out of the Pit*, the compendium of Fighting Fantasy monsters, and *Titan*, the guide to the world of Fighting Fantasy.

This book contains four adventures for you to play. To get the most out of them, you should play them in order, as 'chapters' in a 'story'. However you may, if you wish, decide to play them separately. Before you sit down to play the game, you must decide which one of you is to be the GamesMaster. Once you have decided this, the GamesMaster must read through the adventure to get a good grasp of the story.

It is vital that none of the other players are allowed to read the adventure: if they do there will be no surprises and little excitement for them in the game. Only the GamesMaster should refer to this book and he will decide what the players get to see and learn. The only book the players may look at is *Fighting Fantasy*, which tells them how to create and equip their adventurers.

IF YOU ARE GOING TO PLAY IN THE ADVENTURES, STOP READING NOW!

FOR THE GAMESMASTER

The Riddling Reaver is a being with many guises. Among bawdy yokels, he will seem to be a rumbustious fellow of mirth and merriment. When at the court of some noble, however, he will be full of charm, chivalry and courtly etiquette – the perfect diplomat.

This chameleonic ability has allowed our scheming friend to blend into many communities, where he has gleefully spread chaos and disorder, turned brother against brother, and always escaped justice. All this he did in the name of his masters, the Trickster Gods of Luck and Chance (see *Titan* for more details). But now he is plotting a scheme so grand, so apocalyptic, so downright devious, that the dastardly Balthus Dire would wince with abject jealousy were he to hear of it!

In these adventures, your players will soon encounter the quizzical, enigmatic trappings of the Reaver. While he may seem whimsical, he is not to be trifled with. An unpredictable enemy is a deadly enemy. Still, the adventurers must stop the Reaver if his perilous plan is not to come to fruition and plunge Allansia into Primal Chaos.

Creative GamesMastering

There will be times when the adventurers decide to do something which is not covered by the text. Here you must do some creative GamesMastering (this is explained further on pages 19–20 of *Fighting Fantasy*). To give you some more help, here are a few do's and don'ts:

DO make sure the players understand how to fight and use their equipment *before* the adventure begins, since explaining the rules during the game can be terribly boring.

DON'T get frustrated if the players are not doing exactly what you expect them to; after all, it is *their* adventure.

DO make sure you know what all the magical items, potions and spells do; but don't give their secrets away to the players until it is necessary.

DON'T play too long! It is far better to make the game a series of cliff-hangers than have it peter out.

DO tell your players to keep accurate records of their SKILL, STAMINA and LUCK scores, as well as their possessions.

Restoring STAMINA and LUCK

The four scenarios in this book are packed with hazards, and adventurers may find that they lose STAMINA and LUCK quite quickly. It is important that you give them the opportunity to replenish these scores, otherwise they will die before they get a chance to complete the story.

Both STAMINA and LUCK can be restored by magic (spells, potions or scrolls). They may also be recovered in other ways. STAMINA may be increased by eating Provisions. As explained on page 42 of *Fighting Fantasy*, you should allow adventurers to eat Provisions at any time that they may reasonably do so (in other words, not in the thick of battle). Players should keep track of how many Provisions their characters have by means of their *Adventure Sheets*.

LUCK may be recovered through *Luck bonuses* (see page 40 of *Fighting Fantasy*). If a player comes up with an idea that is particularly fortunate for the adventurers, then you should award them between 1 and 3 points of LUCK. This may never take their LUCK above its *Initial* level.

Equipment

Each adventurer will begin the game with the following equipment:

A sword
A backpack
A coil of rope
10 Provisions
No potions

Note that additional equipment may be obtained during the adventures. All equipment carried by the adventurers should be noted down on the *Adventure Sheet*.

Adventure Structure

To make things easier for the GamesMaster, the story has been split into four separate parts (or Acts, as we have called them). Each Act opens with a *Players' Tale* (which is to be read out) and a *Games-Master's Tale* (which is to give *you* an idea of what the Act is all about). The Acts are split into Scenes, which follow the format used in *Fighting Fantasy*. For example, in Act One, the adventurers race around various locations in Kallamehr, trying to find the items required to fulfil their quest. A set of locations that fit together makes up a Scene. The Scene will be illustrated with a map, showing the locations within it. These locations will have numbered references so that you can find your way around them easily.

Each Scene will have Tasks. When the adventurers successfully complete the Tasks, the Scene is over, and they may proceed to another Scene.

Although the Acts are designed to be played in order, it is possible to play them individually. In some cases you can change the order you play the Acts in, so that Act Two follows Act Three, for instance.

The Players' Tale, and any other section which is printed in italics, is to be read out to the players.

Creatures in the Adventures

While there are a number of new creatures in this book, many more can be found in *Out of the Pit*.

Consult it if you need further details about a monster, or want to introduce other monsters.

Creatures in the adventures will not always fight to the death. One way in which you can be kind to your players is by having monsters flee when they are getting low on STAMINA, or when their allies have been killed.

Unless otherwise stated, all creatures in the adventures have an ATTACKS score of *one*.

New Rules

Here are a few additional rules which experienced GMs may like to add to their games for that extra touch of realism.

Unconsciousness

In a solo Fighting Fantasy book, should your STAMINA score be reduced to zero, then you die. However, since in a multi-player game you have comrades who can come to your rescue, it is fairer to allow you a chance of survival.

So, if your STAMINA should be reduced to zero, you are merely unconscious. If your STAMINA is reduced to −1, then you have been mortally wounded. If your STAMINA is −2 or less, you have been hacked to pieces, and there is no hope for you!

Unconscious characters will wake up after a number of minutes (roll two dice to find how many). When they wake up, they will have 1 point of STAMINA.

Mortally wounded characters require assistance from others. Potions or spells are the only way of reviving a mortally wounded character. These should be used to raise the character's STAMINA above zero. If they are unsuccessful, the poor character has bled to death!

Note that these rules about unconsciousness do not apply to the players' opponents.

Weapons

It stands to reason that hitting someone with an enormous battle-axe is going to hurt far more than poking them with a black pudding. In *Fighting Fantasy* all weapons were treated as the same, to keep the game simple and fast-paced. Some Games-Masters, however, may like to add that extra edge of realism to their games by varying the amounts of damage that weapons inflict. In the system presented below, damage will be determined by rolling a die.

The table below shows the damage done by a selection of death-dealing implements, commonly used by adventurers and monsters alike. To use it, first locate the relevant weapon on the chart. Then read along to find out how the roll of a die will determine the number of STAMINA points lost by the opponent for every successful Attack Round. Note that a sword, an adventurer's standard weapon, still does the usual 2 points, as does a mace (another favourite).

Weapon	Damage Die Roll					
	1	2	3	4	5	6
Battle-axe	1	2	2	2	2	3
Dagger	1	1	2	2	2	2
Mace	2	?	2	2	2	2
Spear	1	1	2	2	3	3
Morning star*	1	2	2	2	3	3
Sword	2	2	2	2	2	2
Two-handed sword†	2	2	2	3	3	3

* Adventurer fights at −1 SKILL
† Adventurer fights at −2 SKILL

For example: Mhagi the Thrasher is wielding a wicked morning star (a spiked metal ball on the end of a length of chain). Since it is difficult to control such a weapon, his SKILL of 7 is reduced to 6. If his Attack Strength is greater than his opponent's, he rolls a die and consults the above table to find out how much damage he does. Suppose he is in a desperate battle with Lord Zlargh: if he rolls 5 or 6, he does 3 points of damage to Zlargh. Pity him if he rolls 1 too many times, though!

In order to speed up combat, you may like to modify ordinary dice so that they give the damage for particular weapons. You could, for example, have a blue die for a spear. You paint out the dots on this blue die until there are two faces with one dot, two faces with two dots and two faces with three dots. Then you can just roll this die to determine the spear's effectiveness, instead of consulting the above table. Do the same sort of thing with different dice in different colours, to use for other weapons.

Certain creatures will use weapons, in which case they will also have the opportunity to roll dice for their damage. If they are using a claw, or some other weapon not listed above, then they will do the standard 2 points, unless their description tells you otherwise.

Mighty Strike

There are times – either by incredible luck or by deft timing – when an adventurer's blow will strike with extra force, or find a weak chink in an opponent's armour. To account for this, GamesMasters may like to introduce *Mighty Strikes* to their game.

A Mighty Strike occurs when a character in a battle rolls double six for his Attack Strength. When this happens, the character *automatically* mortally wounds the opponent (i.e. the opponent's STAMINA is reduced to −1).

Magic

To add extra spice to the adventures, you may allow *one* of the adventurers to be a wizard. Because he has spent so much time poring over dusty tomes, and had so little exercise, this character will have the minimum STAMINA score of 14. Since he has had no training in weapons, his SKILL score will be found by rolling one die and adding 4, rather than the usual 6. However, he makes up for this with an important extra characteristic – his MAGIC score. Roll two dice and add 6. Enter this in a MAGIC box on the character's *Adventure Sheet*. It determines how many spells the adventurer may use *in each Act*. Before the adventure commences, the wizard's player must choose which spells he will have from the list below. Every time he uses a spell he must cross it off his list. He may choose more than one of each spell. Wizards should beware: some spells may not work on some opponents!

Spell-casting – Hit or Miss?

Spells do not work automatically. There is always a chance of failure, even for the greatest of mages. Whenever a wizard tries to cast a spell, he should roll three dice. If the result is *less than* his MAGIC score, then the spell will work correctly. If the result is *equal to or greater than* his MAGIC score, however, something has gone wrong. The GamesMaster should decide what happens: it may be that the spell simply fails; or, worse still, it may misfire and affect the wizard or his comrades. For example, a misfiring Creature Copy spell might create a copy of the wizard himself, who would then proceed to engage the unfortunate sorcerer in a raucous argument about who was the real wizard! Misfires should be humorous rather than deadly – there is enough danger in the adventures already!

Even if a spell misfires, it should still be crossed off the wizard's list.

Certain spells are listed as having a *Standard Dura-*

tion. This means that the GamesMaster should secretly roll three dice when the spell is cast. This determines the number of minutes for which the spell is in effect.

Creature Copy

This spell will allow the wizard to conjure up an exact duplicate of any creature he or his comrades are fighting. The duplicate will have the same SKILL and STAMINA scores, and the same powers, as the original. But the duplicate will be under the control of the wizard's will and he may, for example, instruct it to attack the original creature and then sit back and watch the battle! *Standard Duration*.

ESP

With this spell the wizard will be able to tune in to psychic wavelengths. It will not let him *read* someone's thoughts, but it will indicate general frames of mind. For example, it will tell the wizard whether someone is angry, friendly, honest or hiding something. It is very useful for rooting out impostors.

Fire

Almost every creature is afraid of fire, and this spell allows the wizard to conjure up fire at will. He may cause a small explosion on the ground, which will burn for several seconds and cause its targets to lose an amount of STAMINA determined by rolling one die. Or he may create a wall of fire, to keep creatures at bay (crossing the wall will cause 3 points of damage). The wall of fire lasts for the *Standard Duration*.

Fool's Gold

This spell will turn ordinary rock into a pile of what appears to be gold. However, it is merely a form of Illusion spell, although more reliable. The spell lasts for the *Standard Duration*, after which the 'gold' reverts to rock.

Illusion

This is a powerful spell, but it has its limitations. By means of this spell the wizard may create a convincing illusion (for example, that there is a bridge over a gaping chasm, or that the floor is covered with hot coals) with which to fool *one* creature. The spell will immediately be cancelled if anything happens which dispels the illusion (for example, if someone steps out on to the illusory bridge). An illusion can never lead to the laws of nature being broken – while a creature may receive illusory damage from an illusory sword, it will in fact do no physical damage. It is all in the mind! Even if he becomes unconscious, when he recovers he will find he has sustained no actual injuries.

Levitation

The wizard may cast this spell on to objects, opponents and even himself. It frees its target from the effects of gravity and causes them to float freely in the air under the wizard's control. It is not a Flying spell: the wizard may only move the target up and down. The spell lasts for the *Standard Duration*.

Luck

When cast, this spell will restore an adventurer's LUCK score by half its *Initial* value (if his *Initial* LUCK score is an odd number, then round off the number downwards). This spell can never raise a LUCK score above its *Initial* level. The spell can never be cast while the wizard is in combat.

Shielding

Casting this spell creates an invisible, immobile shield in front of the wizard and up to six companions, which protects them from physical objects such as arrows, swords or creatures. The shield is not effective against magic and, of course, just as nothing outside it can touch the wizard and his friends, so they will not be able to touch anything outside it. The shield lasts for the *Standard Duration*.

Skill

This spell is identical to the Luck spell, except that it works on the adventurer's SKILL score.

Stamina

This spell is identical to the Luck spell, except that it works on the adventurer's STAMINA score.

Strength

This spell has the effect of increasing the wizard's strength to that of a Troll when it comes to heaving, humping and battering (for example, when lifting heavy boulders, battering down locked doors, etc.). The GamesMaster should use his judgement to decide what may or may not be achieved, bearing in mind that using *too much* strength for a task may have disastrous results! The spell will only last for *one* major action (battering one door down, heaving one boulder, etc.).

Weakness

Strong creatures are reduced to miserable weaklings by this spell. The GamesMaster should roll one die twice, first for the victim's SKILL and then for its STAMINA score – this shows by how much these scores will be reduced. The weakness will last for one combat only.

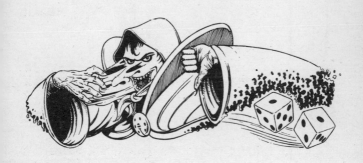

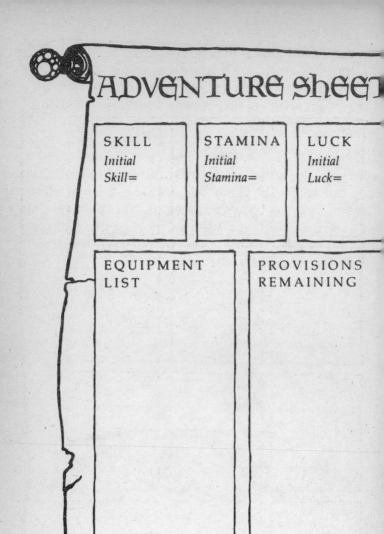

ADVENTURE SHEET

SKILL	STAMINA	LUCK
Initial	*Initial*	*Initial*
Skill=	*Stamina=*	*Luck=*

EQUIPMENT LIST	PROVISIONS REMAINING

MONSTER ENCOUNTER BOXES

Skill = *Stamina* =	*Skill* = *Stamina* =	*Skill* = *Stamina* =
Skill = *Stamina* =	*Skill* = *Stamina* =	*Skill* = *Stamina* =
Skill = *Stamina* =	*Skill* = *Stamina* =	*Skill* = *Stamina* =
Skill = *Stamina* =	*Skill* = *Stamina* =	*Skill* = *Stamina* =

ACT ONE
THE CURSE OF KALLAMEHR

Players' Tale

You have been trekking across Allansia, in search of adventure, excitement – and above all treasure! Forsaking the western shores, you headed south, and came to the land of Kallamehr, which is ruled by the noble house of Rangor. Compared to the hardships you faced on the journey, Kallamehr promises comfort and rich pickings. Judging by the rounded bellies of the traders you have passed on the road, business must be good around here.

After two months' solid travelling, interrupted only by the occasional skirmish with beasts and bandits, you have caught the scent of the sea in the wind. The road broadens as it approaches the town of Kallamehr, and you see its famous tower looming majestically in the distance. As you draw near the town, you catch sight of the sprawling collection of buildings which huddle beneath the tower. The twisting architecture is strange to your northern eyes; it seems to have no order to it. You wonder how on earth people can live in such chaotic squalor.

An imposing pair of gates looms before you. Strangely, no guards seem to be around, and the gates are open. You can make out the faint sound of shouting from the other side of town, but the houses block your vision and you cannot see what the commotion is about.

As you stand in the gateway, you hear thumping from the gatehouse to your left. Someone seems to be trying to attract your attention.

'In the name of charity, let me out!' a tiny voice implores. 'Surely I, one of Baron Bluestone's most loyal subjects, should have the right to witness his struggle? Let me out!'

Edging closer, you see a man's gaunt face pressed against the door's grille. Manacled hands grip the bars, and tears stain his grubby face. He does not look much like a loyal citizen to you, and he has almost certainly been locked in the gatehouse for a good reason. There are no keys near by.

Abandoning him to his fate, you hurry towards the sound of the crowd, which gets louder as you get closer. Carts sit unattended, stalls unguarded, and livestock runs free. Minutes after leaving the gate, you arrive at the central square – the scene of the commotion. Packed into the square is a vast crowd (surely the entire population of Kallamehr, apart from the wretch in the gatehouse!). Each pair of eyes is fixed on the top of the tower, where a spindly figure is struggling to free himself from the clutches of a short robed man, who in turn is trying to force the other off the edge of the balcony. The spindly man is teetering on the edge. With every twist and turn the onlookers gasp ever louder. The tension is unbearable.

GamesMaster's Tale

The scenario begins with the players arriving at Rangor Tower, pride of the wealthy merchant-lords of Kallamehr, just in time to witness the Baron's last moments. Having failed to prevent his death, the players will become embroiled in its aftermath. After investigation they will come across a mysterious box left by the villain, the Riddling Reaver. The box contains a scroll with obscure riddles, by means of which the Reaver sets the characters a challenge: they must assemble three items from the town (the solutions to the riddles) and cast them into the sea at Brion's Bluff, the westernmost tip of the peninsula. So the characters will have to search the town for the items; they will encounter various villains, cut-throats, innocents and traps. The trip round the town will be conducted in one Scene. The players must successfully complete the crucial locations in order to assemble the three items. The adventure ends as these are cast from the cliff, and the players await results . . .

Scene One: Tower Trouble

Tasks: Meet Lady Carolina. Find and open the Riddler's box.

1

You are in the throng of townspeople, struggling to avoid being crushed against the sea wall. People are shrieking in disbelief, and pandemonium reigns. You guess that it is the Baron up there, fighting for his life. But why?

Nobody seems able to do anything; guardsmen are pounding in vain on the mighty oaken doors of the tower. The crowd just stands and stares.

The sea crashes against vicious rocks at the foot of the cliff below the tower. Now is your chance to demonstrate your heroism. Can you save the Baron? But how do you reach him?

The players must come up with some way of reaching the top of the tower. Although ingenious players may think of others, there are three main ways in which this can be achieved. Firstly, they may join in the assault on the doors. This is the least adventurous option. If one of the players is a wizard, he may decide to use the Strength spell to smash down the doors. The players may then enter the tower: proceed to Location 3.

The second option is to scale the walls by means of its ivy covering. If the players ask about the tower, you should tell them that it is covered with a thick growth of ivy, which could be climbed by someone nimble. If the players decide to climb the ivy, go to Location **2**.

Finally, a shrewd wizard player may decide to use the Levitation spell to ascend the tower, or enter a window. He will arrive too late to save the Baron, and will have to cope with the Riddler's devious exit on his own, but he will be able to go down and open the doors for the other characters. The GamesMaster should describe the inside of the tower to the wizard's player alone. Try to keep the description brief – the other players will want to explore these locations more fully on their way up.

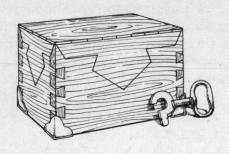

2

You grasp the thick strands of ivy and begin to climb. You can hear the crowd below gasping at your bravery. But it is a long way to the top of the tower . . .

The tower has four floors. For each floor scaled, players must roll against their SKILL. They must roll two dice. If the result is lower than their SKILL, then they have successfully climbed the ivy to the level of the next floor. If the total is higher, then they run out of handholds and can proceed no further. If they roll a double, then they may fall. They should *Test for Luck*. If they are Unlucky, then they will fall. Roll one die, and add 2 points for each floor above the first that the adventurer attempted to climb. The Unlucky character will lose this number of STAM-INA points. If they are Lucky, then they are merely stuck – and must be 'rescued' by another character.

Each of the floors has a large window, through which an adventurer may climb. If the adventurers do not wish to risk climbing all the way to the top, they should tell you which floor they want to enter. Adventurers climbing the tower will enter locations as follows:

First floor	Location 4
Second floor	Location 5
Top of tower	Location 6

3

Beyond the shattered remains of the mighty doors is a short passage, leading to the ground-floor chamber of the tower. The chamber is sparsely furnished, with a rough wooden table and a few chairs. Hanging against the walls are various cooking utensils, and sides of meat. On the other side of the room there is a large fireplace with a chimney-breast. Around the walls of the room, a spiral staircase ascends to a trapdoor in the high, arched ceiling.

Sitting on one of the chairs is a beautiful woman. She is bound, with an expression of utmost horror on her face. Perched on her head is a large glass jar. Swarming in the jar are at least a dozen TARANTULAS! The slightest movement will bring the jar crashing to the floor, releasing its deadly contents.

The adventurers must act quickly! The woman is Lady Carolina, the young wife of Baron Bluestone. She has managed to remain perfectly still despite her terror, but now, with help at hand, she is wavering. Suddenly her nerve breaks and the faintest tremor passes through her. It is enough! The jar falls into her lap . . . and then drops on to the stone floor. It is still intact! Then, as the adventurers watch, it rolls lazily towards the table, strikes a leg, and shatters!

There are fifteen Tarantulas in the jar. Treat the seething mass as one creature:

TARANTULAS SKILL 7   STAMINA 15   ATTACKS 4

When the Tarantulas win an Attack Round, they

do no damage to STAMINA. Instead, they inject their venom. This will affect the victim after one minute, causing black spider-hair to spring up on his body. This growth itches terribly, and is very distracting. The victim will lose 2 points of SKILL until the hair is removed. Further bites have no further effect, though the players do not know this. A Potion of Strength, rubbed vigorously into the body, will remove the hair and prevent it returning. Alternatively, the victim may have to go to the barber's every morning for a complete body-shave!

Lady Carolina will be delirious with terror, crying 'Traitor! I knew there was more to that little rat of a soothsayer!' Should the adventurers tell her of her husband's plight she will fall into a deep faint.

The trapdoor will lead you up to the first floor, Location 4.

4

*The first floor consists of impressive living-quarters,
adorned with rich tapestries and furniture. The floor is
littered with small scraps of paper. The room is gloomy,
since the curtains are drawn and the only two candles shed
a feeble light. On an opulent couch sits a man in the robes
of a wizard. He sits quite still and is apparently deep in
thought. He seems to be smiling broadly, and cradles a box
in his hands.*

This room contains the corpse of Hammet the
Dash, a local wizard employed by Lady Carolina to
discover the source of her husband's torment. Sadly, he was successful. He discovered that the
Baron's soothsayer, one Cona Numdrum, had been
slowly driving Lord Bluestone out of his mind by
bombarding him with riddle upon riddle. Having
entered the tower to warn the Baron, he was inter-
cepted by Numdrum. Revealing himself to be the
Riddling Reaver, agent of the Trickster Gods of Luck
and Chance, the traitorous soothsayer slit Hammet's throat, and left his final riddle – in the box held
by the poor wizard – before hastening to the top of
the tower, to dispatch the Baron.

Hammet is quite dead, his throat slit from ear to
ear. The box he holds is a beautifully crafted piece of
work, made of interlocking sections of some very
hard wood. It will be pointless trying to open the
box without having solved the cryptic instructions
inscribed on its surface.

If you would see what I contain
And maybe learn some news of gain,
Solve this riddle, drop me in it,
Wait for the click, then pull me from it.
I will be open, then you'll see
The reason for this riddle-me-ree:

'It trembles at each breath of air
And yet can heaviest burdens bear,
It shows no mark when it is hit
And more – you're mostly made of it!'

The solution to this riddle is *water* and the box must be immersed in water to be opened – see Ending the Scene, pages 42–4.

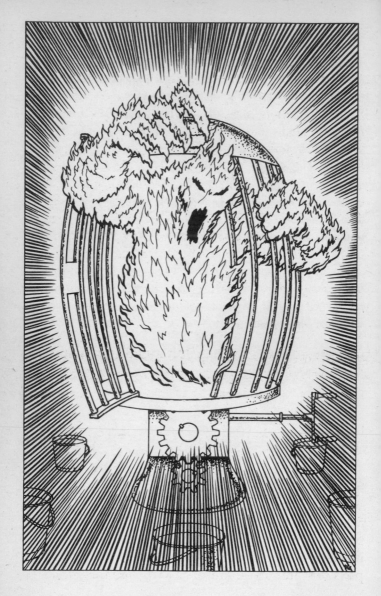

5

The walls of this room seem to be made of silvered metal, and have been polished until they are almost perfectly reflective. The effect of being in a circular room with mirrored walls is eerie, to say the least. The room has larger windows than those of the floor below, and it soon becomes obvious that this room serves as the tower's beacon. The source of light is a large fiery being, held securely in a cage in the centre of the room. The cage, half of which is barred and half walled, stands on a podium which revolves slowly. The light from the creature dazzles you and you cannot look at it directly. You are thankful that it is safely imprisoned behind magically enchanted bars. Stationed at regular intervals around the room are half a dozen pails of water. As the last of you steps into the room, the door of the cage slowly swings open. Someone has been careless . . .

The creature is a DEVLIN, and the adventurers must defeat it before they can leave this room.

DEVLIN   SKILL 10   STAMINA 0   (see below)

The Devlin is invulnerable to earthly weapons, but can singe away 2 points of STAMINA if it wins an Attack Round. It is vulnerable only to dousing. There are six pails of water around the room which may be used to try to repel the Devlin. A character who throws a pail of water at the Devlin must *Test for Luck*. Success indicates that the Devlin has been banished back to the Magical Plane of Fire. Failure indicates a miss. Players who do not think to use the pails of water do not deserve to escape this room!

6

*The roof of the tower is made of rough flint stones. A tall
flagpole in the centre flies the Baron's emblem. As you
arrive you catch a fleeting glimpse of Baron Bluestone
teetering on the parapet of the tower, but then plummeting
to the rocks below. His opponent turns slowly round,
chuckling insanely to himself. When he sees you, he
scampers over to the flagpole. He grips it firmly – and
spins effortlessly up it, right to the top! His voluminous
grey robe billows in the breeze and hides his features. He
cackles at you.*

*'Looks like we're a bit late, aren't we?' he squeals. 'Your
precious Baron's not much use now, is he? He had no
sense of humour, anyway!'*

It may seem that the players have cornered the
evil-doer responsible for the Baron's death. But the
Riddling Reaver (for it is he!) will make good his
escape, in a dramatic fashion. As the adventurers
advance on him, a gasp wafts up from the crowd far
below, and a mighty shadow falls on the tower's
summit. Hovering majestically some twenty metres
above is a vast marrow-shaped flying vessel. Beneath it hangs a small, luridly coloured gondola,
from which trails a rope. The Reaver grasps this,
and pauses to hurl a parting shot to the adventurers.

'I do so hate goodbyes. Maybe we'll meet again
. . . or maybe not.' So saying he pats the top of the
flagpole, and spins up the rope to the gondola.
Within seconds the pole starts to writhe and twist,
transforming magically into a GIANT SNAKE,
with its tail still firmly planted into the roof. The

Snake will attack anyone who remains on the roof, but cannot follow them down the trapdoor.

· GIANT SNAKE   SKILL 7   STAMINA 11

If the Snake scores two hits in succession, it will swallow its prey whole, and he will quickly die.

Meanwhile, the Riddling Reaver will have glided off into the wild blue yonder, leaving the inhabitants of Kallamehr shocked and stunned.

Ending the Scene

However they fare in the tower, the adventurers should be left with the mystery of the box to solve. The solution to the riddle is *water*. If the players do not seem to be able to guess it, the GamesMaster should help them – maybe Lady Carolina could guess it? To be opened, the box must be completely immersed in water. If it is, a loud click will be heard, and when the box is removed it will fall open – though its contents will be perfectly dry. There is no other way to open the box than this; it will resist all efforts to smash it open. Inside is a parchment on which is written the following:

I always believe in giving people a chance. After all, without Chance there is no Luck, and without either where would I be? You can try to follow me, if you want to avenge Bluestone's death. And I won't stop you. In fact, I'll provide the transport. But to pay your fare, you'll have to gather three trinkets and feed them to the God of the Sea at Brion's Bluff. What's more, the trinkets aren't even hidden. All you have to do is solve my riddles to find where in Kallamehr they are. I hope you're lucky. Then again, I hope you're unlucky. It's all the same to me.

What am I?

A white-winged fish that parts the waves,
I ply the sparkling waste.
I'm bound by ropes, and pulled by cloth,
Lest merchants lose their haste.

Where am I?

My first is in south but not in north;
My second is in picture but not in play;
My third is in fourth and also in worth;
My fourth is in book and also in cook;
My fifth is in toe but now in sew;
My sixth is in life but not in death;
And together I'm found where children abound.

What am I?

My belly is round
And bound with iron bonds;
What I carry always raises a cheer.
Murder have I not done;
Stolen not; cheated not;
Yet a peg is beaten into my head.

Where am I?

My coat is green and I can speak
Of several things, but mostly cheek.
In such a prison I am set
That has more loopholes than a net.

What am I?
I've neither top nor bottom,
Yet I hold bone and skin;
I hardly ever make a noise,
And yet my name's a din.

Where am I?
Ill-matched is my visage to my frame —
Horns are on my head, the rest a hideous man;
By fame well known through all the Allansian
lands;
From man and beast together is my name.

The Riddling Reaver

You should copy these riddles out and give them to the players, so that they can refer to them in the next Scene, 'About Town'.

For your information, the answers to the riddles are as follows:

Answer 1: The item is a *ship*, and it is to be found at the *school*.

Answer 2: The item is a *cask*, and it is to be found at the *'Parrot in a Cage' inn*.

Answer 3: The item is the *ring* which is worn by the *Minotaur*.

Scene Two: About Town

Task: Find the three items – the ship, the cask and the ring.

1

The death of Baron Bluestone has sent shock waves throughout the city-port. Bewildered locals are grouped here and there, recounting the tragic events that you were a part of. It is up to you to see that justice is done! Somewhere in the town lie the solutions to the Reaver's riddles, and to stand any chance of catching up with him, it seems you must play his little game.

You are still in Rangor Tower. The Lady Carolina agrees to supply you with any weaponry you may need in your quest. She will send out to the armoury to supply you with fine arms, crafted by the best weapon-smiths in Kallamehr.

She also arranges for a guide for you. Hammet the Dash, the unfortunate wizard who was killed by the Riddling Reaver, had an apprentice. Dappa is only fourteen, but has an intimate knowledge of the city. He will be able to give you guidance and seems very keen to help you with the riddles.

You should give the players a free choice of weapons to add to their characters' Equipment Lists.

Dappa is a useful character for you to play. He will enable you to give the players hints about which directions to go in if they are having trouble. Dappa is a short, mischievous individual with a quick

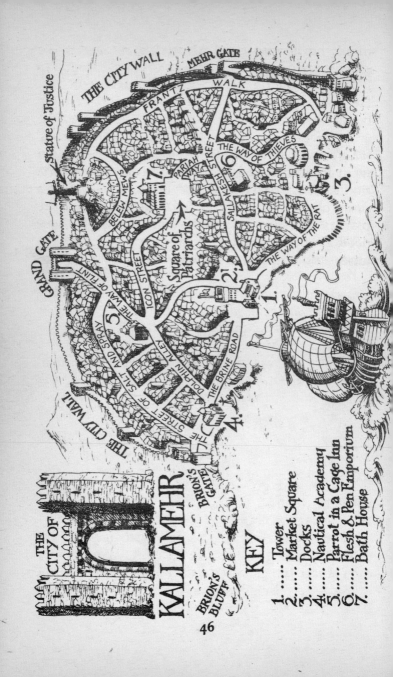

THE
CITY OF

KALLAMEHR

BRION'S BLUFF

46

KEY

1. .... Tower
2. .... Market Square
3. .... Docks
4. .... Nautical Academy
5. .... Parrot in a Cage Inn
6. .... Flesh & Pen Emporium
7. .... Bath House

mind: he is very good at solving riddles! If the players are getting stuck, you should use Dappa to help them. But he will not just volunteer solutions. He will want to demonstrate how smart he is by being obscure. He will give clues to the solution, and be very disdainful about any 'stupid heroes' who cannot solve 'simple riddles'. Whenever you want to give the adventurers a bit of help with a riddle, consult Dappa's Clue Table, which gives a series of clues for each riddle. Give the clues to the players in order. Hopefully your players will not need too many clues. You should not over-use the table: it does not do to let players get lazy!

Dappa's Clue Table

Ship:
1. *'I can tell you're landlubbers.'*
2. *'Take a look in the harbour, what do you see?'*
3. *'Pish, pish, you should rearrange my words, dummies!'*

School:
1. *'It's easy if you've been there.'*
2. *'It rhymes with another word for idiot – which is what you are!'*
3. *'What has a pupil, but isn't an eye?'*

Cask:
1. *'If you're to accomplish your task, make me rhyme.'*
2. *'You'll often see this fellow rolling along streets and into taverns.'*
3. *'I'd have thought you'd have got this one! You drink enough of what's inside it!'*

Parrot in a Cage:
1. *'What talks, but can't argue?'*
2. *'It's a pet, numskulls!'*
3. *'Pieces of Eight, Pieces of Eight!'*

Ring:
1. *'It's got no ends, and it's often precious.'*
2. *'It's only a little thing, but it can bind two people together.'*
3. *'It's round, but you can put your finger through it.'*

Minotaur:
1. *'I think he's cheating — it's not a place, it's a person!'*
2. *'I'm a-mazed you can't get this one!'*
3. *'The only way to solve riddles is to take the bull by the horns and tackle them like a man.'*

If it comes to a fight, though, Dappa will change his tune and want protection: he's no warrior! The only spell he learned from Hammet was Invisibility; he will try this in an emergency, but only on himself.

DAPPA   SKILL 4   STAMINA 8   MAGIC 8

Dappa explains that the best place to begin investigating will be outside in the market-square. From there, the players will be able to choose where they go. Show them the map of the town so that they will see the locations of most interest. Whichever of the major locations they aim for, they must pass through the residential area (Location 8).

Whenever the characters find one of the three items, they will hear a manic cackle from the Riddling Reaver's parchment, and the riddles relating to that item will mysteriously fade away.

2

Even the death of Baron Bluestone does not prevent the traders making their daily living, and the market-square is busy. Exotic goods, fine cloths and succulent foodstuffs adorn shops, stalls, carts and barrows. Business is brisk, and the locals have little time to take notice of strangers.

As you pass through the throng, a cry goes up. The crowds part as a lanky, ill-formed youth shoulders his way through, wildly swinging a vicious-looking cudgel. Behind him, sprawled in a quivering heap, you can see a rich merchant. There is no room to draw a sword, and even if you did you would risk hurting innocent bystanders.

The thief is making directly for the adventurers, and they must make a snap decision to get out of his way or to apprehend him. If they decide to try to stop him, they may not use weapons, and will fight at a penalty of −4 to SKILL.

LARGO THE SWIFT   SKILL 6   STAMINA 10

Should Largo be beaten, the merchant will recover his purse and thank the adventurers profusely. He will introduce himself as Ignatius Galapagos, a trader who deals exclusively in exotic livestock for discerning customers. He proudly boasts that he supplied the monsters for Baron Sukumvit's Trial of Champions – the notorious Deathtrap Dungeon. He moans about the ill fortune that has beset him ever since he landed in Kallamehr: the scurvy rogues who were handling his cargo have slid away, taking with them his famed exhibit, a Minotaur with the ability to snort poisonous gas through its nostrils!

3

The docks are dirty, dark, smelly and full of the shadiest characters you have ever seen. Mysterious robed figures loiter on every corner and you have the distinct feeling that unseen eyes are watching your every move. As you approach the large wooden storage barns which line the waterfront you stop in your tracks. The barn door furthest from you creaks open, and two shady figures emerge, manhandling what appears to be a body. They drag it to the quayside and drop it into the sea. As they slide back towards the barn, you hear shouting from inside the huge building.

The building houses a hastily constructed arena. A large pit has been dug, and its sides built up with barrels and loose timber. Every available inch of seating around the rim is taken up by an assortment of sailors and rogues, all clutching coins and yelling bets at one another. They are so absorbed in the spectacle that they will take no notice of the adventurers if they enter the barn. At one side of the rim stands the master of ceremonies, resplendent in an enormous turban and garish silk pantaloons. As the adventurers approach the pit, he will yell: 'Who dares challenge the mighty Minotaur of Mellizand? Is there anyone brave and hardy enough to last the turn of the sand-glass? Come now, surely 100 Gold Pieces make it worthwhile?'

In the pit fumes the strange beast, brought to Kallamehr by Ignatius the merchant. It has been abducted by the crew of the ship which Ignatius chartered, and they are using it for cruel sport. Anyone who looks into the pit will see a rather pathetic-looking Minotaur – certainly nothing like the mighty beast of legend. In his nose he wears a brass ring. This is the ring the players seek, and the only practical way to get it is for one of the adventurers to volunteer to fight the beast.

MINOTAUR SKILL 9   STAMINA 9   ATTACKS 2

The brass ring in his nose enables the Minotaur to breathe a stinking cloud of poisonous gas every four Attack Rounds. Characters caught in the cloud must *Test for Luck* or lose 4 STAMINA points. Lucky characters will lose only 1 point.

The sand-glass referred to by the master of ceremonies times a period of seven Attack Rounds. If, after this time, a character is still up and fighting the Minotaur, then a rope will be let down, so that he may climb out of the pit and claim the prize. He will be given a bag of coins (the sneaky ringmaster has put only 74 coins in it, however), and told that he may not fight the Minotaur again.

If they are to recover the ring, another one of the adventurers must fight and defeat the beast!

An adventurer who defeats the creature will have just enough time to recover the ring from the Minotaur's snout before three angry thugs jump down into the pit and attack. The audience of rogues will have melted away, and the beturbaned ringmaster will be nowhere to be seen. The lone victor will need help from the rest of the party! Each of the three thugs has the same characteristics:

THUG   SKILL 6   STAMINA 5

4

The Nautical Academy of Kallamehr is an ancient and decrepit building. It is perched dangerously close to the cliff, and you wonder what prevents it from sliding into the sea! Robed children career noisily in and out of the large entrance and lean out of windows. At the top of the building is an ancient weathervane in the form of a ship. Perched precariously on this is a grubby youngster who attracts your attention by lobbing loose bits of tile at you.

Kallamehr's school for aspiring young sea-captains is famous throughout this region. Equally notorious is its reputation for harbouring some of the most rebellious, mischievous brats in the area.

The weathervane in the shape of a ship is one of the items which the heroes are seeking. If they are to recover it, they must find some way of getting it down, either by magic, or simply by climbing. While the intricate architecture of the building will make it easy to find handholds, the roof is badly decayed, and the children will also be doing their best to hamper any climbers.

In order for a character to reach the weathervane, the player must first roll lower than his SKILL to reach the roof, and then again to scale the tiles. If either of these fail, then the character cannot reach his goal, and risks falling, thanks to the tiles thrown by pupils. He must *Test for Luck*. If he is Unlucky, then he will fall. Roll one die and subtract the result from STAMINA. If a character falls while crossing the roof, then he will have fallen through the tiles and into the classroom beneath.

If a character successfully makes the climb, by the time he reaches the top, the young rascal will have made his escape by sliding down the tiles and swinging into a window.

To get the character down, the player must again make the SKILL rolls.

Smart players may try to bribe or coax the children into helping them remove the ship. Ingenious players should be able to come up with a number of schemes, and it is up to you, the GamesMaster, to decide how successful these will be. Bear in mind that these little villains are no softies!

If the heroes decide to venture inside (or fall through the ceiling!), then read the following description:

The building houses one enormous classroom, filled with decaying desks and musty books and charts. It is in uproar. Rival groups of pupils seem to be conducting mass warfare against one another, and soon you are embroiled in a battlefield of water-bombs, ink-pellets, peas and other more unsavoury missiles. Slumped on a desk at the front of the class is the portly shape of the teacher. He is caked in dust, and is clutching a half-eaten apple. Tied to its stem is a note: 'To Sir, from yore beluvved pueples.'

All attempts to wake the teacher will fail – he has been drugged by his 'beluvved pueples'! He will remain asleep no matter what.

If any adventurers are foolish enough to take a bite from the apple, five minutes later they will doze off, and will remain asleep for the rest of the Scene!

There is nothing else of interest in the room.

58

5

The 'Parrot in a Cage' inn is the most successful, and the most disreputable, drinking-establishment in Kallamehr. Dappa warns you of its infamous clientele, and he enters with reluctance. Inside the smoky den, a large crowd of assorted ne'er-do-wells are massed around a table. A cocky young man is performing a trick with three shells and a pea. Two piles of coins testify that this is no idle game. You soon notice that nobody seems able to beat the man at his game. It looks simple, and he shuffles the shells very slowly, but somehow he manages to deceive all comers. There is only one person in the inn who does not seem to be very interested in the game. He is a short, rat-faced fellow who sits by the bar, playing with his bead necklace, and occasionally muttering to himself. By his head hangs a slate with the prices of ale; it can be bought by the tankard or by the cask. Behind the bar you can see casks, bottles and barrels untidily stacked.

As you look around, your faithful guide Dappa urgently gestures for you to follow him outside. There he explains that the rat-faced man was once an apprentice of his former master, Hammet the Dash. He was dismissed for petty thievery, which he accomplished using magic. Unless he is very much mistaken, Rat-face has something to do with the young conjuror's amazing run of luck.

Rat-face is, in fact, influencing the game by means of his magical necklace. He has arranged to split the proceeds with his accomplice. No one has made any connection between the two, so it is up to the players to decide the fate of these con artists.

They may decide to ignore what is going on, and press on in search of the cask (which can be purchased at the bar for a paltry sum – the 'Parrot in a Cage' is certainly *not* famous for the quality of its ales!).

Alternatively, they may decide to expose the trick first. They will no doubt come up with a plan for this – or even a way of profiting from it! It is up to you to decide the results of these actions. However, the most likely choices will be either publicly to denounce the scoundrels, or to prevent Rat-face's magical interference and join in the game (where they will find it easy to outwit the youth) and win Gold Pieces to the value of three dice rolls.

Explaining the trick to the inn's proprietor will lead to the two con men being dragged off to court for a dose of Kallamehr's vicious justice. The innkeeper will thank the adventurers profusely, and shower them with drinks. He will even give them a whole cask of ale to show his gratitude!

If an adventurer takes Rat-face's bead necklace, it will add 1 point to his *Initial* LUCK score for as long as it is worn (unless the character is a wizard, in which case it will add 2 points).

6

The Flesh and Pen Emporium is a gaudily decorated building. Its walls are covered with designs for lurid tattoos. Judging by the nautical flavour of many of the pictures, the Emporium is a favourite of sailors. Standing just outside the entrance to the building is a burly fellow. He wears only a loincloth, and is covered from head to foot in tattoos. He has attracted a small crowd of admiring street urchins and passers-by, to whom he is demonstrating the unique qualities of his designs. As he flexes his right arm, the tattoo of a belly-dancer comes to life, while on his left, a fearsome cobra rears and strikes. The interior houses even more of these fabulous works of art. Some of them have been drawn on thick parchment, others adorn what looks like flayed skin! Busily at work on his latest masterpiece is a craggy old Dwarf who must be well over two hundred years old. His willing victim is whining pitifully as the Dwarf's needles prick his flesh. With a final flourish, the tattoo is complete, and the shaken sailor staggers over to a full-length mirror. The design is of a blazing sun beating down on a tropical island.

'With this enchanted tattoo, my friend, you will never catch cold again!' croaks the Dwarf. The sailor grimaces.

'I should think so too, after all I've had to endure!' he mutters, slipping on his shirt and departing.

None of the Reaver's items are hidden in the shop, but the player characters may be persuaded by the Dwarf to invest in some bodily decoration. If they are *really* keen they may even have one of his fabled magical tattoos, which bestow strange powers on their wearers. These are not cheap, however.

While a normal tattoo can be had for a Gold Piece or two, magic ones cost 25 Gold Pieces. Adventurers may choose from the following tattoos:

Rising Sun. As described above. This enables the wearer to endure the lowest temperatures without ill effect, and to withstand the fiercest winds and downpours. Very useful for sailors.

Leaping Tiger. A striped cat springing out of jungle foliage. Bestows the power of ferocity. If a character calls upon this power by revealing the tattoo, then he will add 1 point to his SKILL for as long as the tattoo is visible. What is more, he will be able to fight on for one round *after* his STAMINA falls to zero. He will suffer the ill effects only *after* the battle.

Eagle. A majestic hunter of the skies. Gives the power of sharp sight. The bearer can see great distances, and will be able to notice things that most people would overlook.

Cobra. A hooded serpent poised to strike. Enables the character to mesmerize an enemy. If the wearer exposes the tattoo, the victim must roll two dice. If the total is less than or equal to his SKILL, the opponent is unaffected. If the total is greater, however, he will stand transfixed for one Attack Round – and the tattooed character may inflict a wound automatically. This ruse will work only once on any one opponent.

A character may wear only *one* of the magic tattoos. The tattoos can never be removed.

7

Made entirely of gleaming white marble, the Kallamehr bath-house is clearly the place to be if you are rich and idle. Located in a prosperous area of town, it boasts an enormous pillared entrance – large enough to accommodate its stouter patrons!

Inside, a simple entrance lobby is attended by a snooty-looking individual in a ceremonial bath-towel. He peers at you disdainfully, and asks:

'Am I to assume that you are not members? I hardly think that our members would dress themselves in such a slovenly fashion.'

Non-members are not ordinarily permitted to use the baths, but the attendant will explain that he is prepared to make an exception in their case, as long as they pay the 'nominal fee' of 5 Gold Pieces. Dappa points out that it is a rare privilege to enter the baths, and the influential members of the Bath-house Club may be able to help them with their quest. If the players decide to explore the bath-house, read the following:

Before entering, you must remove all your clothing and weaponry, which is taken to the cloakrooms by a servant. All that may be worn in the baths is a towel. You are directed to the pool, which apparently lies at the end of a maze of passages. You meet no one on the way, but after a short walk find yourselves in front of a pair of brass doors. Inside is a small bathing-room. Steps lead down from the door into the sparkling waters. Across the room are an identical pair of brass doors.

If any of the players have tattoos then they will be clearly visible – and magical ones will take effect.

The particular pool to which the adventurers have been directed is one used for the entertainment of the bath-house's patrons. When the adventurers have all entered the pool, the brass doors will swing shut. Looking up, they will see that they are being watched from a balcony. Several bloated individuals are gazing down arrogantly. As they reach the centre of the room, the onlookers will begin to empty large pots into the pool. From the pots descend cascades of water and . . . ELECTRIC EELS! Each of the six eels has the following attributes:

ELECTRIC EEL   SKILL 6   STAMINA 4

Each Attack Round, *one* of the eels will let off its electric discharge, doing 4 points of damage to the adventurer it is attacking. Each eel can emit only two bursts. You must choose which adventurers are affected.

The brass doors through which the heroes entered have been locked, leaving the other doors as the only means of escape (the walls of the pool-room are smooth marble, which cannot be scaled). Unfortunately, the doors lead straight out into an alley round the back of the bath-house. The bath-house fatties will be roaring with laughter at their joke. If the adventurers somehow manage to defeat the six eels, another six will be thrown down.

The heroes will find that their belongings have been scattered about in front of the bath-house, causing much humiliating laughter from passers-by!

8

Kallamehr is a large sea-town, though quite unlike the dark and treacherous ports of the north. You soon realize that although it looks chaotic, it is actually very well ordered. Its streets are clean, and its citizens seem quite contented with their lots.

You need read this to the players only once, although they will undoubtedly pass through the residential areas between locations several times. Each time they do, you should roll on the following Residential Area Encounter Table:

Residential Area Encounter Table

Roll two dice and consult the table to discover what the adventurers meet on their way through the town.

Dice Roll	Encounter
2	A trained KRELL (a six-armed monkey – SKILL 8, STAMINA 5) will attempt to pick the pockets of one of the adventurers. If the adventurer has the eagle tattoo, he will notice instantly. Otherwise he must *Test for Luck*, and be Lucky to avoid losing all his Gold.
3	One of the adventurers (decide by rolling dice) will be falsely accused of theft. Six guards will attempt to arrest the character. If the adventurers remain calm, and insist that the guards consult the Lady Carolina, then all will be well,

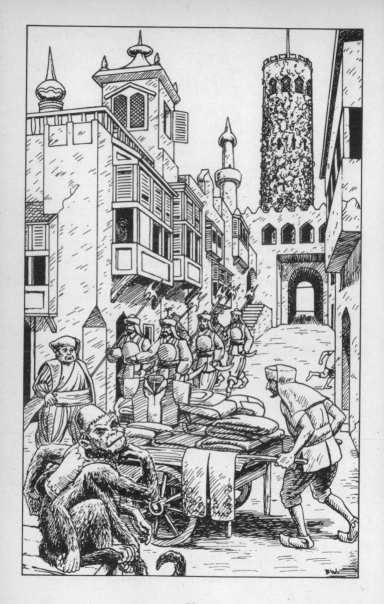

and they will quickly be released. If they attack the guards, however, then they will have committed a crime, and will have to fight any guards they may later meet. Any guard is SKILL 6, STAMINA 5.

4–5   The adventurers meet a guard patrol. If they are wanted for a crime (see encounter above), the guards will attempt to arrest them. Otherwise, they will ask the adventurers if all is well, and whether they have seen anything amiss.

6   A street-trader attempts to sell the adventurers some of his wares. They may buy new clothes off him, if they wish, but must carry them in their backpack. A complete set of clothes costs 1 Gold Piece.

7   No encounter.

8   The adventurers are mobbed by urchins. Word has got about that they are on a heroic quest for the Lady Carolina, and these admiring young ragamuffins want souvenirs. To get rid of the urchins, each adventurer must part with one item. Otherwise, the party will be surrounded by screaming, yelling street urchins for the rest of this Scene!

9   The adventurers bump into Ignatius Galapagos (see Location 2). If they helped him then, he will hail them for a

chat, and ask if they have seen his Minotaur. If they have not, he will shrug, and offer them 5 Gold Pieces each by way of a reward for catching the thief – it had slipped his mind at the time! If they have seen the Minotaur, he will be keen to know where it is. If told it is dead, he will start to weep uncontrollably, and hurry off, saying he must go to the bath-house.

10–11 The adventurers run into a vicious street gang, armed with knives, and intent on murder and theft. They must fight! Six members of the gang attack: each is SKILL 7, STAMINA 4. If half of their number are killed or knocked unconscious, the rest will run away.

12 The adventurers are attacked by a PRESS-GANG! Half a dozen heavies (each SKILL 6, STAMINA 8) set upon them with cudgels. If all the adventurers are knocked unconscious, when they awake they will find themselves on board ship. They will have little choice but to work for the notorious Captain Sanbar. They have failed in their quest for the three items. However, the quest for the Riddling Reaver can continue! Captain Sanbar's ship can be wrecked, and the adventurers washed ashore on a jungle coastline. You can then run Act Three.

Ending the Scene

Once the adventurers have assembled the three items, they should hurry off to Brion's Bluff. Read the following to the players:

A mighty storm assails Brion's Bluff as you approach the cliff's edge. Waves crash against the rocks far below. It is an ominous evening. As you hurl the ship, the cask and the ring out to sea, the storm seems to become yet more frenzied. The clouds brew overhead. You can do nothing but stand and wait . . .

This is the end of Act One, 'The Curse of Kallamehr'. It leads directly on to Act Two, 'Voyage of Enigma'. If you are going to continue with the story, you must decide what happens to Dappa. He is very keen to continue adventuring, even though he is not as skilful as the adventurers. They must decide whether they want him to come along with them. If they refuse, he will return, sadly, to Kallamehr.

If he accompanies them, you must continue to play him yourself. He may come in useful for giving clues and hints, so use him to guide the players smoothly through the story. If given a weapon, he will fight to the best of his ability. But he has one weakness – he is terrified of spiders and creepy-crawlies! If he encounters any, he will start shrieking with fear, and will lose any weapons he may be carrying.

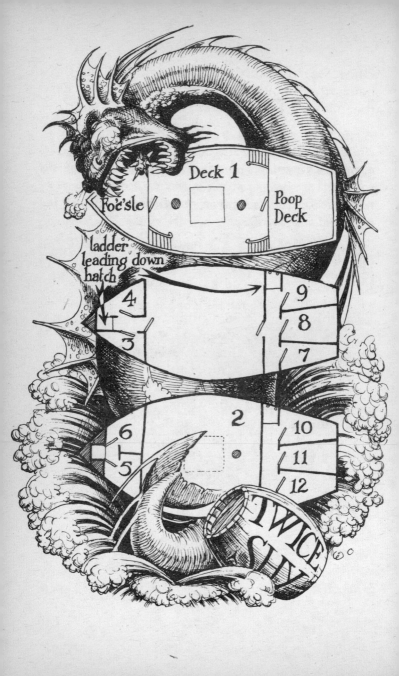

ACT TWO
VOYAGE OF ENIGMA

Players' Tale

You are on the trail of a mysterious opponent, the Riddling Reaver. This servant of the Trickster Gods of Luck and Chance has murdered a great nobleman, and must pay the consequences. His motives for the crime were obscure, but his behaviour suggests it was part of some greater plan. Your quest has brought you to a tall cliff on the coastline. As the stormclouds boil and rage overhead, and the furious wind lashes you, you sense that this turmoil is but a fragment of some greater battle on a Higher Plane. Are you destined to be a part of that battle?

You wait for minutes that seem like hours. Then, looking out to sea, you catch sight of a sail. But what kind of ship sails in a storm like this? As it approaches, the winds abate and the waves crash less violently against the rocks at the foot of the cliff.

You see the familiar shape of a merchant's galley gliding towards the cliff. But this is no ordinary trading vessel. For you can see no crew on its deck. Its sails hang lifeless from its masts, yet the ship glides smoothly over the waves. As you look closer, you see that the galley really is sailing over the waves – it is floating above the water!

Suddenly, the ship stops dead. A landing-boat is winched down to the waves, and moves towards the shore. Again, you are certain that there is nobody aboard. It reaches a narrow cove just along the cliff from you, and grinds on to the sand. You get the feeling it is waiting . . . for you.

A slippery path leads down to the beach from the top of the cliff, which you can easily descend with a little care. As soon as you all climb into the boat, it slides down into the water, and smoothly heads in the direction of the galley. What have you let yourselves in for?

GamesMaster's Tale

The Act opens with the adventurers boarding the *Twice Shy*, the Reaver's sea-going vessel. Once they have boarded it, the galley will sail off at great speed, following the coastline across the Glimmering Sea. Its journey ends after it crosses the Gulf of Shamuz and reaches the jungle coast. The adventure takes place entirely on the ship, and therefore consists of only one Scene. The only important Task to be accomplished by the adventurers on the ship is to stay alive until the journey is over! However, there will be much to occupy them on the *Twice Shy*, as the riddling villain has left plenty of traps and menaces to test our intrepid heroes.

This scenario is designed to be run with a time-limit, representing the duration of the sea voyage. You should decide beforehand how long you want the game to last. When the time-limit is up, allow the adventurers to finish what they are doing (if they are in the middle of a fight, for instance!) and go straight to Ending the Act, pages oo–oo.

The scenario begins with the landing-boat being winched up on to the deck of the galley. You should therefore start off at Location 1, the deck.

Most ships' decks are very cluttered with ropes, barrels and all kinds of nautical tackle. Not this one, though. There is not so much as a coil of rope. The deck seems to be made entirely from black pine, one of the strongest and rarest woods in Allansia. In its middle, between the masts, is a hatchway, presumably leading to the hold. At each end of the lower deck there is a door. To the right of the forward door is a large brass plaque, on which is inscribed 'Twice Shy'.

Even on the upper decks, there are no ropes – nor even a wheel for steering! What wind there is seems not to touch the sails: they hang limp and lifeless.

The deck has no inhabitants, but that will not necessarily prevent the adventurers from encountering something!

The first time they are on the deck, after having climbed out of the landing-boat, there will be nothing here, and they will have to choose from the doors at each end of the ship and the deck hatch to proceed further. However, on subsequent visits (or if they refuse to leave, preferring the coward's option of staying put), they will find that the deck is not quite the haven of safety it might seem. There are several possible encounters here. Whenever the adventurers venture back on the deck, you should roll one die and consult the Deck Encounter Table to see what they have met. Roll again if the encounter has already happened – each one can only occur once.

Die Roll	Encounter
1	A huge PLESIOSAURUS (SKILL 9, STAMINA 22) rears its ugly head out of the sea and swims towards the *Twice Shy*. Not surprisingly, it is quite hungry. If the adventurers are able to satisfy it by throwing it plenty of food, then it will go away. Otherwise they will have to fight.
2	A mighty storm assails the ship. Although the *Twice Shy* is in no danger of capsizing, the adventurers may be less secure. For out of the storm will swoop 1–6 STORM SPIRITS, fierce elemental creatures, children of the raging skies: each is SKILL 10, STAMINA 6. Though wingless, the Storm Spirits fly at terrifying speed. Before the battle commences, you should ask each of the adventurers which weapon they are going to use. Make a note of which characters are using metal weapons. Each Spirit can unleash up to two bolts of lightning. These bolts hit on a roll of 1–4 on one die, and do 2 points of damage. Also, anyone using a metal weapon who wins an Attack Round against a Storm Spirit will lose a point of STAMINA due to the Spirit's electric power.
3	Another ship approaches from directly ahead. With horror, the adventurers will see that it has black sails – it is a plague

ship . . . or worse! As it passes the *Twice Shy*, several of its occupants leap across. They are PLAGUE ZOMBIES, horrific undead creatures who suffer from the dread Plague of Undeath.

1–6 Plague Zombies (each SKILL 5, STAMINA 7) will leap across as the ships pass. A further 1–6 will try to leap, miss and end up in the sea. Pity the poor shark who tries to make a meal of one of them! Anyone reduced to zero STAMINA by a Plague Zombie will be given the disease. After five minutes they will rise up, reborn as a Plague Zombie!

4   Looking ahead of the *Twice Shy*, the adventurers can see a slow old merchant ship, sailing into their ship's path. Try as they may to divert the path of the *Twice Shy*, there is nothing they can do. The enchanted vessel charges straight into the merchant ship, splintering it in two as if it were balsa wood, and then continuing straight on. The trader's cargo and crew are unceremoniously dumped into the sea. The poor shipwrecked sailors must fend for themselves.

5   The adventurers see what appears to be a
Sea Snake slide over the side of the ship.
You should ask them what they intend to
do, and get a quick reaction from them. If
they run for one of the deck's exits, they
will avoid the encounter successfully.
Otherwise they will have to contend with
an enormous GIANT SQUID, which is
questing for food. It is SKILL 9, STAMINA
12, ATTACKS 2. The Squid will attempt to
entrap adventurers in its coils. If it wins
any two successive Attack Rounds, it will
squeeze its victim for an extra point of
STAMINA loss. If the adventurer wins the
next Attack Round, he has broken free,
and normal combat is resumed; if the
Squid continues to win, it will continue
to cause 3 points of damage. Although
the Squid can normally capsize large
vessels, it will find the *Twice Shy* too
difficult. If there is no food to be found
on the deck it will give up and sink back
beneath the waves.

6   A huge blue-skinned SEA GIANT,
some nine metres tall, looms over the
side of the ship and questions the
adventurers: *'What puny land-dwellers are
you to taint my realm? If you would pass,
then tell me this: Which is more powerful, the
wind or the sea? And why?'* The
adventurers must reply that the sea is the
more powerful of the two, and give a
convincing reason (use your
judgement!), otherwise the Sea Giant
will attack: it is SKILL 10, STAMINA 17,
ATTACKS 3. If the correct answer is
given, the Giant will laugh, send a huge
wave crashing over the *Twice Shy* (this
will drench the adventurers), and dive
beneath the sea.

All the other locations in this scenario are below
the decks of the ship. These should be treated in the
same way as rooms in a dungeon (as in *Fighting
Fantasy*). Remember, the adventurers will require
some kind of light to see further than one metre in
the darkness.

2

Beneath the lower deck of the boat is a large cargo hold.
Edging down the ladder, you find yourselves in the quiet
darkness of this storage area. Peculiar smells assail your
nostrils, and the damp warmth of the hold feels strangely
alive. Hanging from the rafters is an unlit lantern.
Littered around the floor near by are barrels. One of these
has fallen on its side and its contents – salted fish – have
spilled out. Towards the aft part of the hold you can dimly
make out a large packing-case. Forward there seem to be
half a dozen smaller cases, stacked together. You can hear
the occasional soft skittering noise – probably rats.

There are four barrels near the ladder, including
the one which has fallen over. All four barrels
contain salted fish. However, one of them also
houses a rat, which will leap out as the barrel is
opened, biting the opener for 1 point of STAMINA
damage, before racing off into the shadows. The
barrels' contents are of little use, but may be used to
appease the Plesiosaurus should the adventurers
encounter it on the deck. Alternatively, they may
eat the salted fish. As it is rather unpleasant to taste,
eating as much as can be stomached will restore
only 2 STAMINA points at one time.

If they wish to, the adventurers may take the
lantern. It is full of oil.

The six small packing-cases forward are quite
unremarkable to look at, though each one carries a
branded stamp saying, 'For the Attention of Captain Redlen Reiver'. Their lids are crudely nailed on,
and can be prised loose with the edge of a sword.

The first box contains a beautifully made, full-size, glass right arm. The next case contains a left arm, the others contain left and right legs, a torso and a head – all exquisitely crafted from flawless glass. If all the pieces are assembled, the head will glow with an inner light as the MANIKIN is activated. This ingenious device is another of the Reaver's play-things. It will respond to simple spoken commands, and carry them out to the best of its ability. How-ever, there are disadvantages: it will obey com-mands literally, since it has no intelligence; it will always follow the *last* command given; and it is not choosy about whom it obeys – it will try to follow *any* order it receives. If it is involved in a battle, and its STAMINA is reduced to zero, then it will shatter.

MANIKIN   SKILL 8   STAMINA 3

The adventurers will discover the Manikin's func-tion only if they say anything which it can take as a command. When not being commanded to do something, the artefact will remain perfectly still.

If the players approach the packing-case at the other end of the hold, you should read them the following:

The packing-case is about two metres tall, and three metres long. Written on its side is a riddle:
'What has the head of a jungle king, the body of a hill-climber, the tail of a legless lizard and the breath of a winged hoarder? The answer's in the box!'

Sure enough, in the box is a CHIMERA, which will spring out and attack if the box is opened.

CHIMERA   SKILL 12   STAMINA 20   ATTACKS 3

The Chimera will bite with its lion's head, kick with its goat's hoofs, and constrict with its serpent's tail. It can also (every three Attack Rounds) breathe a gout of flame at one opponent. This will hit on a roll of 1–4, doing 2 STAMINA points of damage. The Chimera cannot get out of the hold on its own, as it cannot fly and is too heavy for the ladder. If the adventurers have trouble defeating it, they may find it advisable to escape up the ladder to the 'safety' of the deck.

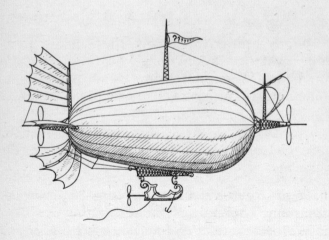

3

The door opens easily, and you find yourself looking into a smallish, sparsely furnished cabin. A sturdy hammock has been lashed between two stout timbers, and an unlit lantern hangs from the ceiling. Around it dangle various types of fish. They are all neatly stuffed, and tied to the rafters with pieces of string. This cabin's former occupant clearly felt more at home under water! In the centre of the room is a large box, at least a metre high, which is clamped to the floor by iron bands. There is a stool in front of it, and it has two small holes bored into its side – apparently eyeholes.

The stuffed fish are just what they seem. The lantern may be taken by the adventurers; it is full of oil. The box is a Casket of Visions, designed by the Riddling Reaver for his guests as a form of amusement during the tedium of the voyage. The first adventurer to look through the eyeholes will see a curious sight. You should take the player aside and secretly read the following:

Inside the box there is a golden glow. When your eyes have adjusted to the light, you see that the box is filled with gold, gems, jewellery – more than you have ever seen in all your years of adventuring!

In order to get into the box, the adventurers will have to smash apart the iron bars. This will take some time – at least ten minutes. During this time it is likely that one or more of the other players will want to look at the contents themselves. You should ask the players whether they are looking into the

box. Each one who does should be taken aside and told a *different* tale of its contents, so that each adventurer will have very different views on whether or not to open it! Below are the alternative visions to be seen within the box. Each player's vision will remain the same, no matter how many times they come back to the eyeholes to look.

Vision 2
At first you can see nothing in the box but darkness. Then a chill runs down your spine as two eyes open and stare back at you. They burn with a seething malevolence, a chill fire that must surely come straight from Hell.

Vision 3
The inside of the box seems to be moving. When you look closer, you see that there are thousands of insects — termites, spiders and other loathsome creepy-crawlies. From this writhing mass a skull protrudes. It has been picked clean.

Vision 4
Your eyes adjust to the darkness, and you make out the cramped figure of a beautiful maiden, bound from head to foot. She is gagged, but her eyes clearly convey her terror. You do not know how long she has been imprisoned here, but it looks as if she cannot last much longer.

Vision 5
Sitting inside the box is another box, finely crafted of interlocking pieces. It has some writing carved on its surface, but you cannot quite make out what it says.

If the players finally decide to open the box and succeed in smashing the iron bands, the lid will fly off and a loud squeal will be heard. A creature (actually a huge jack-in-the-box!) will shoot up from the box and tower menacingly above the adventurers, swaying to and fro. You should describe this to the players, and ask them what they are going to do. Should they attack it, then they will hack it to pieces very quickly. If they leave it alone, however, it will give them a hint: *'Gluttony has proved the downfall of many a brave adventurer.'* After saying this, it becomes a lifeless dummy. There is nothing else in the box.

4

*Set into the wall is a portal with no door. All you can see is
a sheet of darkness within the door-frame. Drawn around
the frame are hundreds of little stick figures, engaged in
curious activities, such as running, jumping and wrap-
ping their legs around their heads.*

The entrance to this cabin is a Portal of Darkness.
Adventurers may pass through it easily enough.
However, one effect of the portal is that any living
thing passing through it will be shrunk down to the
size of a large beetle. Coming back out through the
portal reverses the process. Moreover, the trans-
formation occurs without the victim noticing anything amiss. If the adventurers enter the cabin, then
read the following:

*Impossible as it may seem, you find yourselves in a vast
subterranean chamber. Its ceiling is so far above your
heads that it is hardly visible. Ahead of you lies dense
purple shrubland. Beyond that, you can make out four
mountainous pillars rising high into the sky.*

What the players are actually seeing is a beetle's-
eye view of a very ordinary cabin. Like most of the
cabins it has a hammock and a small desk. The
purple shrubland is actually a plush carpet, while
the four pillars are the legs of the desk. If the players
advance through the undergrowth, they will have
to hack their way through to proceed. After travelling through the undergrowth for a few minutes, the
adventurers will see a terrifying form coming towards them – a huge grey beast, larger than an

elephant, with four legs and vicious teeth. It is a MOUSE, and the adventurers must fight it!

MOUSE   SKILL 10   STAMINA 16   ATTACKS 2

If they kill the Mouse, the adventurers may continue their exploration. The only item which may be of interest to them will be an enormous golden ingot. The adventurers should *Test for Luck*. If any of them are Lucky, they will spot this glimmering among the undergrowth (an adventurer with the magical eagle tattoo from Act One will automatically spot it). Since it is a metre long, it will take all their strength to heave it out of the room. Of course, once through the portal the adventurers will grow, but the ingot will remain the same size. It is a sliver of gold worth roughly 2 Gold Pieces! So much for easy riches!

5

The door to this cabin opens easily, and you find yourselves in a small dining-hall. A long table runs along the middle of the chamber. It is set for dinner, and a mouth-watering meal is laid out along it. There are cuts of meat, fine breads, soups and dips, and a magnificent centrepiece – a huge silver platter with domed lid. What succulent dish lies inside?

The food on the table is perfectly edible, and is the equivalent of three sets of Provisions. Inside the central platter, however, is something far less tasty.

Swarming within are several hundred FLESH GRUBS. These hungry flesh-eating maggots will make straight for the person who lifted the lid. Although blind, they have an unerring sense of smell, and will be able to wriggle their way towards any adventurer. The unfortunate who lifted the lid will be covered by 2–12 Flesh Grubs immediately, and more will spill towards him unless he runs for it. Each Flesh Grub will automatically inflict 1 point of STAMINA damage as it nibbles away at the victim. They can be pulled off and crushed quite easily. A further 2–12 Flesh Grubs will latch on to their original victim and anyone else, if they are foolish enough to remain near the table.

While the adventurers were preoccupied with the table and its contents, an IMITATOR slid down from its perch above the door they came through, and reformed itself in the shape of the door. If the adventurers take the sensible option and flee from the deadly Flesh Grubs, they will stumble into the disguised Imitator.

IMITATOR   SKILL 9   STAMINA 8

When the victims touch the Imitator, they will stick fast, held by a glue-like substance secreted by the creature. At the same time, it will strike with a large, fist-shaped protuberance. The trapped prey can fight back, but with SKILL reduced by 2. Once the 'fist' is cut off (Imitator's STAMINA reduced to zero), the creature is defenceless. It can be finished off rapidly and the glue will lose its potency. However, if the fight takes more than four Attack Rounds, Flesh Grubs will start arriving at a rate of 2–12 per Attack Round!

6

The door opens into a cabin. There is a small, but comfortable-looking bunk against the wall, and a writing-desk with a stool across the room from the bunk. The floor is carpeted and the walls are painted bright blue. The cabin looks as if someone has been here recently: there are clothes strewn about the place, and papers litter the desk.

This cabin formerly belonged to Bhorriz, a wise seer whom the Reaver befriended. They frequently used to dispute the nature of the world and ruminate upon metaphysics together. Then Bhorriz came up with the perfect solution to the world's problems – a system of government which would ensure that peace and goodness would spread throughout the lands of Allansia, and perhaps beyond. The Reaver realized that this would upset the balance between Good and Evil, so he threw the seer overboard. He never got round to tidying up the cabin.

The GHOST of the unfortunate seer still inhabits the cabin. One minute after the adventurers enter the cabin, a spectral form will materialize and begin to moan at them. If the players decide to attack it, they will find that their weapons pass straight through it. After moaning for a minute or so, the Ghost will start to whisper insistently:

'You must not be fooled by him, no, no, no . . .'

If the adventurers try questioning Bhorriz, he will explain further:

'You are all pawns in a cosmic game. Luck and Chance determine the outcome, and they are jealous of their

power. You must not play the game, no, no, no . . . The countervailing equipoise is not yet come to fruition . . .'

He will carry on in this vein for as long as the players are prepared to listen to him. Most of what the poor, demented old spirit says is complete rubbish. If asked how he came to die, he will briefly explain the circumstances of his death, and then return to his philosophical ramblings. The only other piece of useful information the adventurers will be able to extract from the Ghost is the solution to the riddle on the door of the Riddle Room. If they ask him how to get into the room he will tell them:

'Just say, "The answer is a riddle", and the door will open.'

The papers on the desk are Bhorriz's notes. Their contents are on the same lines as his whispered comments – mostly unintelligible intellectual jottings. Hidden among them is a Scroll of Fortune. Reading this has the same effect as drinking a Potion of Fortune. As the letters disappear from the page when read, the Scroll can be used only once.

In the pockets of Bhorriz's clothes are 10 Gold Pieces.

7

This cabin is well furnished, though covered with a thick layer of dust. Judging by the thick silk tapestry and opulent armchairs, it belonged to the ship's master. There is a dresser with a mirror on the far side of the room, near the bunk, which is enclosed by velvet curtains. A drawer of the dresser is slightly open. On the walls hang a selection of cutlasses, a cat-o'-nine-tails, and various torture implements. To your right there is a rough wooden perch.

As the adventurers enter the cabin, the drawer of the dresser will loudly slam shut. If they examine the mirror, they will find that someone has written 'Lay my bones to rest!' in the dust. While they are looking in the mirror, they will see the bed-curtain open in the reflection. From the bed will climb a crusty old sea-captain. His right leg is a wooden stump and on his shoulder sits a mangy green parrot. If the adventurers turn to face him, they will discover that there is no one there, and the bed-curtain is undisturbed!

If they open the bed-curtain, they will find a skeleton – or rather two skeletons, one of a man (whose right leg is missing below the knee), and the other of a bird, which lies by the first skeleton's shoulder.

If the players attempt to open the drawer of the dresser, the cutlasses, cat-o'-nine-tails and torture instruments will fly off the walls towards the adventurers. Each must successfully *Test for Luck* to avoid losing 1 point of STAMINA. The weapons are thrown by a POLTERGEIST. This is the spirit of the former pirate captain of the *Twice Shy*, who was foully slain by the Riddling Reaver: hot lead was poured down his throat. He is furious at being kept so long in limbo, and desperately wishes to be buried at sea, so that he may at last attain rest. After throwing things at the adventurers, he will pick up a cutlass (since he is invisible, they will be able to see only the weapon, waving in the air) and attack.

POLTERGEIST SKILL 9 STAMINA 0 (see below)

The Poltergeist cannot be harmed by mortal weapons, and will fight until either the adventurers are driven out of the room, or his bones are taken from the bed and thrown over the side of the ship.

During the battle, one or more of the adventurers may have the gumption to try to move the bones. If they do so, a ghostly parrot's voice will squawk, 'That's the way to do it!', and the Poltergeist's cutlass will stop in mid-air.

If someone manages to carry the bones out of the room, on to the deck of the ship, and to hurl them into the sea, then the apparition of the sea-captain will appear fleetingly and mumble his thanks. You need not roll on the Deck Encounter Table while the adventurers are performing this service.

Under the skeleton's pillow is an eye-patch. This has been enchanted so that the eye it covers can see perfectly in the dark. In normal light, it can mysteriously be seen through, but has no special abilities.

In the drawer of the dresser are some doubloons, worth 20 Gold Pieces.

8

This is quite a large cabin, and contains assorted maps, charts, sextants and other navigational paraphernalia. The cabin is dominated by a huge table, on which lies a map of the whole of southern Allansia, skilfully modelled in three dimensions. Looking closer, however, you can see that where the Plain of Bones should be, there is a ball of fur, about the size of a cabbage, snoring contentedly. You can also make out a small model of the Twice Shy, *in a larger scale than that of the map, which seems to float just above the map, near the coast.*

The players have found the Reaver's map-room. The miniature ship follows the exact course that has been plotted for it beforehand. It in turn steers the *Twice Shy*. If the miniature ship is tampered with in any way, the real ship will be affected. For instance, if an adventurer were to prod the model, then the ship would lurch violently, and the party would be thrown across the cabin, losing several points of STAMINA in the process. The GamesMaster should be able to guess what would happen if someone were to treat it even more roughly! But hopefully the adventure will not end altogether at this early stage.

The ball of fur which is currently sleeping on the Plain of Bones is a JIB-JIB, and belongs to the GENIE which controls the map and ship. If the adventurers wish to examine the room's contents further, then they must tiptoe very quietly (see *Fighting Fantasy*, page 61) to avoid waking the Jib-Jib. If they are successful, then they will be able to help themselves to various valuable instruments

and charts (roll two dice and multiply the result by ten to find their value when sold to a merchant).

If the Jib-Jib is woken or attacked, then read the following description:

The dormant bundle of fur suddenly springs to life, and a fearsome scream rents the air. You look around in terror, expecting to see some vicious monster behind you. There is nothing, and you realize that the banshee yell comes from the timid-looking ball of fur. This terrified creature is now running around the map on its two short, stumpy legs, coming dangerously close to the model of the Twice Shy.

The adventurers must decide whether to leave the room, hoping the Jib-Jib will calm down in their absence, or to try to silence it themselves. If they leave, the caterwauling will continue for a minute or so, and then begin to die away, as the little creature settles down to sleep again. Otherwise, the players must choose between killing or capturing the beast.

JIB-JIB   SKILL 1   STAMINA 2

Any player who says he is trying to capture the Jib-Jib should *Test for Luck*. If he is Lucky, then he has caught hold of it. Several players may say they are trying to capture it, but you should make sure you know which adventurer finally manages to grab it. Alternatively, if the players opt for combat, make sure you know who dealt the killing blow.

Once the Jib-Jib has been caught or killed, a mighty Genie will materialize in a puff of purple smoke. He is extremely annoyed at the treatment of his beloved pet – and if it has been killed he will be bursting with fury. In booming tones, he will address the adventurer who caught or killed his pet:

'A thousand curses upon you, treacherous infidel! For this crime against my companion, you shall henceforth assume a guise more suited to your mischievous nature!'

With this, he unleashes a bolt of flame, which strikes the guilty party squarely between the eyes. There is a flash, and the next instant the adventurer has become a monkey! The Genie laughs and vanishes in a cloud of noxious green gas.

The poor adventurer will still have all his senses and intellect, but they are encased in the body of a small ape:

PLAYER CHARACTER   SKILL 6   STAMINA 4
MONKEY

The monkey cannot speak, though it may well gibber excitedly and gesture its intent.

If the adventurer had merely captured the Jib-Jib, the curse will wear off after half an hour (keep track of the time, and tell the player he is back to normal when the time is up). If the Jib-Jib was killed, however, the curse will be permanent, unless the adventurer can find a way of curing it (a powerful wizard, or even another Genie).

This cabin seems to be a gallery. Pictures on the walls mostly depict heroic battles and scenes of daring. On the far wall hangs a larger painting, covered by a black cloth. The floor is carpeted, and there is no other furniture.

There are paintings for each adventurer. Although different, each depicts a scene in which some hero of legend is in mortal danger. Roll a die once for each adventurer, ignoring 6 and any numbers already rolled. Note down which painting corresponds to each adventurer: this will be useful later on. If the adventurers enter the cabin, you should read out the detailed description of each painting to the player to whom you have assigned each picture.

Picture 1
A smoking battlefield is littered with corpses. Two exhausted figures remain standing, locked in deadly combat; a vile black-plated Demon is about to slice his wicked axe through the shattered remnants of a noble warrior's shield.

Picture 2
A striking aerial view of the top of a crumbling tower, where a fair damsel is being torn from the grasp of her grievously wounded lover by a fell beast of the skies.

Picture 3
A kind-faced lord sits at his table, sharing a meal with his barons. He is just about to drink from a chalice of wine. In the background, a weasel-featured manservant peers from an alcove, clutching a small phial of black liquid.

Picture 4
A callow, inquisitive youth is reading from a magical grimoire. Behind him, a shadowy form seems to be materializing from a swirling cloud of vapour. Its form looms above him; he seems oblivious to its presence.

Picture 5
A handsome, but unkempt adventurer is groping through a grille in a dungeon floor, searching for a muddy sword which has fallen through. Under the grille lurks a Gonchong – the most feared parasite known to man!

The picture at the far end of the gallery is a portrait of the Riddling Reaver (any characters who played Act One will recognize him). If uncovered, it will come to life, and speak to the adventurers:

'Don't try to move, my curious art-lovers! I see you've taken an interest in my collection. Perhaps you'd like to examine them A LITTLE CLOSER!'

Then wild laughter fills the room and there is an intense burst of blinding white light. When the adventurers recover they will each find themselves in one of the scenes depicted in the paintings! They will appear in the painting you had previously noted down for them. You should then take each player aside and ask them what they are going to do. In order to escape from the painting, they must change fate, as explained for each picture below. If they do not, then they will be frozen in the painting!

Picture 1: The adventurer must prevent the blow from landing.

Picture 2: The beast must be attacked so that it releases the maiden.

Picture 3: The adventurer must leap on to the table and knock the poisoned wine from the king's hand.

Picture 4: The book must be slammed shut to dispel the summoning of the Demon.

Picture 5: The adventurer must pull the explorer's hand from the grille.

In order to succeed at any of these, the adventurer must roll under his SKILL on two dice.

Any players who are successful will have saved the fate of the picture's hero, and will find themselves back in the gallery. They will have gained 3 points of LUCK. Any adventurer who failed will be clearly visible in their picture, which will also show the ruin of its hero. The only way they can be freed is if the portrait of the Reaver is turned so that it faces the wall. The portrait (now inanimate) can easily be damaged, but this will not help an adventurer rescue his stranded comrades.

Set into the wall is what seems to be a portal, but there is no door – just blackness. Above the portal is written: 'Only those who lie may enter safely.'

This is a Portal of Darkness. It can be passed through with perfect ease. Any adventurer experimentally poking something through will find that it passes through the darkness with no resistance. However, one metre beyond the door is a pendulum axe, swinging from the ceiling. Anything which is poked over a metre through the Portal will be hit by the axe. The lowest point of the axe's swing is one metre off the ground, so the only way to get through safely is to lie on the ground (hence the notice), and crawl through. Anyone stepping through the Portal without taking these precautions will be hit by the axe, losing 1–6 points of STAMINA. Once the adventurers are inside the room, read out the following:

You are in a small cabin, with a hammock slung from the rafters, and a desk set against the wall. Spread around the room is a menagerie of stuffed animals – cats, exotic birds, snakes and deep sea fish. They litter the floor and even fill the hammock. They are very lifelike: it is as if they have been frozen in time! Sitting on the desk among a collection of stuffed mice are two labelled bottles. On one you can read 'Balm for Curing', while on the other is written 'Balm for Sealing'.

This room is used for taxidermy – the practice of preserving dead animals. It is one of the Riddling

BALM
FOR
CURING

BALM
FOR
SEALING

Reaver's hobbies, and he has perfected it to a fine art. His method involves the use of two potions – the balms that are to be found on the desk. The 'Balm for Sealing' will cause any wounds or blemishes to vanish, and if taken by an adventurer will act as a healing potion, restoring STAMINA to its *Initial* level (there are two doses in the bottle). The 'Balm for Curing' (of which there are three doses in the bottle) is used to preserve a creature. If taken by an adventurer it will toughen his skin. This will increase *Initial* STAMINA by 3 points, but decrease *Initial* SKILL by 2 points, because the skin becomes inflexible. These effects can be cancelled only by a Potion of Strength or a Potion of Fortune (and these will have no effect on the adventurer other than removing the effects of the curing balm).

11

The walls of this cabin are lined with double bunk beds. It is clearly the living-quarters for the ship's crew. And sure enough, sitting at the table in the middle of the room are six grubby sailors, concentrating on a game of cards. Piles of gold on the table in front of them show that the game is for high stakes. They do not seem to have noticed you.

The crew of the *Twice Shy* have an easy life. Since the ship steers itself and requires no hands on deck, her crew can spend their days gambling endlessly. Or so it seems. If the adventurers look very closely at the sailors, they will notice glazed eyes, and a slight stiffness of the limbs. The crew have been stuffed! The Reaver has set up this happy little scene for his amusement. The Stuffed Sailors will carry on playing their game, without batting a glass eye at the adventurers, *unless* their gold is touched. This disrupts their pattern, and sends them into a berserk rage, proving that it is sometimes better to let sleeping dogs lie – especially stuffed ones! They will draw their barbed sailor's knives and attack. Each of the six sailors has the following attributes:

STUFFED SAILOR	SKILL 6	STAMINA 10

If the adventurers survive the battle, they may take the gold; there are 80 Gold Pieces on the table.

There is little else of interest in the cabin, though adventurers may be tempted by a large jug of grog on the table. One swig of this potent brew will restore 2 points of STAMINA. However, further gulps will lower SKILL by 1 for the rest of the Act.

12

The door to this cabin is locked, though there is no keyhole. Above it, a sign reads 'The Riddle Room'. On the door is written:

> *When I appear I seem mysterious,*
> *But when explained, I'm nothing serious.*
> *When I'm unknown to you, I'm something*
> *But when I'm known to you, I'm nothing.*
> *In Master's name you'll me espy,*
> *So tell me, then, please: What am I?*

Listen carefully to what the players say once they've heard this. The answer to the riddle is 'a riddle', and this is the key to the cabin. So if any of the players mention the word 'riddle', the door will swing open. The players may not even know how they opened the door!

You should then read them the following description:

What little furniture you can see in the cabin is of the finest quality. However, it is buried under huge piles of scrolls. Scrolls cover the sumptuous bed at the far end, the delicately carved writing-desk and much of the thick carpet. Only a large black wardrobe is not covered with paper, and that is because it reaches right up to the ceiling.

The room is the Riddler's private sanctum. The scrolls, naturally, are covered with riddles. The players may like to pick a few and have a go at them, if they fancy their riddle-solving abilities. But these are no ordinary scrolls: the riddle must be solved within one minute (you should time this from the moment you give them the riddle to solve), otherwise the scroll will explode. Anyone in the room will be caught in the explosion, and must *Test for Luck*. If they are Lucky, they will lose only 1 point of STAMINA. However, if they are Unlucky they will lose 3 points of STAMINA.

If a riddle is solved correctly, then the words of the riddle will fade from the page, to be replaced by magical lettering. This will be titled, making clear its magical powers. You should roll a die: on 1–2 the scroll will be a Scroll of Skill; on 3–4 a Scroll of Strength; and on 5–6 a Scroll of Fortune. When read, these have exactly the same effects as the potions of the same name, but are good for only one use, since the magical lettering fades as it is read.

When the players pick up a scroll to solve a riddle, you should decide which riddle is on it by rolling on the Riddle Tables (see below). These give a selection of riddles with their answers. When you have found which riddle the players must solve, you should read it to them slowly, so that they can copy it down. The players may make as many guesses at the solution to the riddle as they can in one minute.

If the adventurers open the door of the wardrobe, they will be engulfed in a billowing cloud of smoke. When it clears, a GENIE will be standing in front of the wardrobe, waiting patiently. If questioned, he will explain that he is the Genie of the Wardrobe: it is his duty to look after his master's garments. He will offer to look after the adventurer's clothes, proudly boasting that he can wash and press them in less time than it takes to read a riddle. If any adventurers are foolish enough to give the Genie their clothes, he will disappear back into the wardrobe with a laugh, and the door will slam shut. If the adventurers attempt to persuade the Genie to grant them a wish, he will explain that he cannot disobey his master, as he is a servant of the Trickster Gods of Luck and Chance. The best he can do is to cancel any one misfortune that has happened to the adventurers since they got on the ship. If an adventurer has been turned into an ape by the Genie of the map-room, then he can be cured. Or if a character has been killed in battle, the Genie will be able to bring him back to life. You should use your judgement in deciding what the Genie can and cannot do; you should not let the players get away with anything too outrageous. Once he has granted this wish, or finished talking to the players, he will stream back into the wardrobe in a cloud of gas.

If the Genie is disturbed a second time, he will be angry and irritable. Questions and requests from the adventurers will make him even worse, and he will start turning adventurers into beasts, putting their heads on the wrong way, etc., until the adventurers get the hint that he wants to be left alone. You should use your imagination in thinking up likely curses that the Genie might bestow upon persistent adventurers.

Riddle Tables

First roll one die. If the result is odd, use Table A, otherwise use Table B. Then roll another die to find the riddle. Roll again if you have had the riddle before.

A

Die Roll	Riddle	Answer
1	What has a face, but no mouth?	A clock
2	What has a neck, but no head?	A bottle
3	What has four fingers and one thumb, and is neither fish, flesh, fowl or bone?	A glove
4	What is it that has four legs, one head and a foot?	A bed
5	What runs all day and all night, and never stops?	A river
6	What is it that goes uphill and downhill, yet never moves?	A road or path

Die Roll	Riddle	Answer
1	If you feed it, it will live; if you give it water, it will die. What is it?	Fire
2	What kind of ear cannot hear?	An ear of corn
3	What has four legs and a back, but cannot walk?	A chair
4	What gets wet as it dries?	A towel
5	The more you take away, the larger it becomes. What is it?	A hole
6	What comes once in a minute, twice in a moment, but not once in a thousand years?	The letter M

Ending the Act

When you want to end the adventure, simply read the following out to the players:

Suddenly there is a jerk, and you are all thrown forward. You realize that the ship has stopped dead. While you are picking yourselves up off the floor, you notice a strange, noxious smell. A foul green gas is rising from the boards beneath you, and you start to choke as it reaches your mouths.

To escape the choking gas, the adventurers must make their way on to the deck and off the ship. Fifty metres away is a beach, beyond which rises dense jungle. If the adventurers pile into the landing-boat, then it will automatically be winched down, and it will move steadily towards the beach under its own power, wait for them to disembark, and then return to the *Twice Shy*. Alternatively, the adventurers may like to swim. The tropical waters are infested with SHARKS, and three will attack any swimmers. Anyone fighting in the water will do so at −2 SKILL. Each Shark has the following attributes:

SHARK	SKILL 7	STAMINA 6

The Act will end with the tenacious heroes marooned on the beach, watching the *Twice Shy* floating gracefully off to its next port of call. The Act leads on to Act Three, 'The Pendulum of Fate'. However, if you have already played Act Three, it could easily lead on to the final Act, 'The Realm of Entropy'. Simply amend the introduction as required.

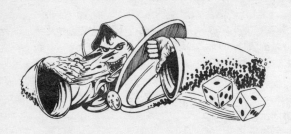

ACT THREE
THE PENDULUM OF FATE

Players' Tale

You are on the trail of the Riddling Reaver, a dastardly villain whose peculiar behaviour seems to serve the ends of Luck and Chance. By a strange turn of fate, you find yourself marooned on a beach. Inland, a dense tropical jungle stretches as far as you can see. Eerie cries and screams come from its depths, and a haze of steam rises into the clear blue skies.

As you consider your next move, there is a horrific scream. Suddenly something flies out from the forest, high above you. A terrifying howl comes from it, as it arches out to sea and plummets into the water. It all happens so quickly that it takes you several seconds to realize that what you saw was a man! Looking out to sea, you notice sharks' fins converging on the spot where the poor soul hit the water.

Soon afterwards, the same thing happens again – a man comes flying out of the jungle and into the sea. This time you can see roughly which part of the jungle the man came from; you could easily make your way there. Since the man was not winged, and seemed unable to control his flight, he must have been catapulted by someone or something. But why?

THE JUNGLE TREK

The Act begins with the adventurers witnessing the horrible deaths of several explorers. When they enter the tropical jungle, they soon come across a gang of vicious mutant Lizard Men. They are killing a band of explorers, and as the adventurers arrive, they are about to catapult the last unfortunate into the sea. When the players rescue him, they discover that his mission was to recover a priceless artefact from a shrine hidden in the depths of the jungle. He agrees to help the party reach the shrine, and warns that he was attacked by the Riddling Reaver, who he believes controls the mutant Lizard Men. However, unknown to the players, he *is* the Riddling Reaver in disguise, who wishes to trick the characters into getting a vital magical artefact, the Pendulum of Fate. He plans to use it to attack Good and Evil – a plan which will plunge Allansia into confusion and benefit his masters, the Trickster Gods of Luck and Chance.

After a series of encounters in the jungle, the characters will arrive at the shrine. This living labyrinth was placed here by the gods to protect the Pendulum of Fate, and because of its magical nature no agent of the gods may enter. The adventurers may enter, however, and combat the terrors within. They should retrieve the Pendulum along with other treasures. The adventure ends as the Riddling Reaver steals the Pendulum from the party, reveals his true identity, and makes a dramatic escape.

To start the first Scene, the adventurers must arrive at the clearing in which the Lizard Men are torturing their victims. If they have any pity, the players will decide to do this on their own. If they seem unwilling to approach the clearing, you (through Dappa, if he is still among the party) should point out that they are stranded, and that finding someone who can guide them through the jungle may be their only hope of survival. You should then go to Location **1**.

Scene One: Nightmare in Green

Tasks: To reach the shrine successfully and enter.

1

You force your way through the jungle, guided by despairing wails. Finally you reach the edge of a clearing and gaze upon a horrific scene. A band of five grotesque Lizard Men are using a winch and rope to bend back a palm tree which has been stripped of its foliage. They are poking and jeering at their prisoner, a ragged and pathetic-looking man whose hands are securely bound. It looks as though he will share the fate of his companions unless you can come to his aid.

The Lizard Men are twisted mutants. The Riddling Reaver captured a number of 'normal' mutant Lizard Men and made their mutations even more exaggerated. They now act as his servants.

They will not actually catapult their last remaining prisoner into the sea (since he is their master in disguise), but they will make all the preparations, so that the adventurers believe him to be in grave danger.

The Lizard Men are wearing the usual spiky armour of their race, and they are all twisted and gnarled. The badge they wear is quite distinctive: it is a double-headed arrow, the insignia of the Trickster Gods of Luck and Chance. Each Lizard Man starts with the same ability scores, though these may be affected by his particular mutation, which you should roll up on the Mutant Lizard Man Table.

126

MUTANT LIZARD MAN   SKILL 9   STAMINA 9

Mutant Lizard Man Table

Roll two dice, and consult the table to determine the special characteristic of each of the Reaver's mutants.

Dice Roll	Mutation
2	Two mutations! Roll the dice to find two different mutations.
3	Skin-shedder. The Lizard Man can rapidly regenerate by shedding its damaged skin. Weapons do it half damage (rounding down).
4	Prehensile tongue. The Lizard Man has a long, powerful tongue which it can use to throttle opponents. Each time it wins an Attack Round, it can do an extra point of damage by constricting with its tongue.
5	Hypnotic gaze. Adventurers must *Test for Luck* when exposed to the gaze, with failure indicating that they are rooted to the spot for *one* Attack Round, during which the Lizard Man will be able automatically to inflict 2 damage points, if no other adventurer intervenes to prevent this.
6	Teeth-spitter. The Lizard Man has a shark-like array of teeth, some of which it can spit at an opponent from a

distance. Before battle commences, it will loose off a number of teeth. The adventurer must *Test for Luck* to avoid losing 1 point of STAMINA.

7 Colour-changer. The Lizard Man changes colour at will. This has no effect on combat.

8 Barbed tail. The Lizard Man has a viciously spiked tail, which it uses in the manner of a mace. It will have an extra attack each round.

9 Slime-spitter. The Lizard Man spits a corrosive slime at its opponent. The adventurer must roll under his SKILL on two dice to dodge the slime. If he fails and it hits, it will do no damage initially, but will do 1 point per Attack Round thereafter. To remove the slime, the adventurer must spend a round wiping it off, during which he will be defenceless.

10 Sulphur-steamer. A cloud of noxious purple steam seeps from the Lizard Man's skin. This irritates the eyes and spoils the aim, so an adventurer will fight at −2 to his or her SKILL.

11 Plague-carrier. The Lizard Man carries a mutant virus which may infect anyone it bites. If an adventurer is wounded by such a Lizard Man, he should *Test for Luck*. If Unlucky, then an hour after the battle he will start to mutate! Roll on this

table to see what the mutation is. His body will alter to accommodate the change (for example, he may have to grow a tail). Any human who has mutated will be hated wherever he goes, and will be run out of most towns. The mutation may only be cured by powerful magic.

12   Multi-headed. Roll a die. If the score is 5–6 then the Lizard Man has three heads, otherwise it has two. Add 1 point to the Lizard Man's STAMINA and SKILL ratings for each extra head. These Lizard Men are very intelligent, and use whips in battle. Whenever one wins an Attack Round, the adventurer fighting it must *Test for Luck*. If Unlucky then his weapon has been torn from his grasp by the whip. He must fight on at −4 SKILL unless he has another weapon, or another player gives him one.

If the five Lizard Men in the clearing are defeated, and the man rescued, he will urge the adventurers to hurry away from the clearing, for there are more Lizard Men about and they are sure to return soon. He leads the way to another clearing, further into the jungle. This is Location 2.

2

The man you have rescued introduces himself as Waxley Speed, explorer and treasure-hunter extraordinaire. *He is very grateful to you for rescuing him from the Lizard Men. In return, he says, he can lead you to a jungle shrine, that people say contains a fabulous treasure. He learned about it when he was given an ancient map by a dying friend. He assembled a band of explorers and spent five years searching and overcoming great perils, only to be thwarted at the last hurdle. This morning, as they were preparing for the jungle trek, a strange flying vessel loomed overhead. Not long after, they were ambushed by a band of Lizard Men. Their leader was a man swathed in robes, whose manner of speech was rather unusual. He stole the map of the shrine, and hurried off, leaving half of his Lizard Men to torture and kill the unlucky explorers.*

Waxley tells you that he has a good memory, and has memorized the map. He can lead you to the shrine if you are willing. He believes it is the resting place of the Pendulum of Fate. This obscure artefact is said to give control over Good and Evil.

Waxley Speed is the Riddling Reaver, who has changed his appearance to fool the adventurers into entering the shrine (something he is magically prevented from doing) and retrieving the Pendulum of Fate, which he needs for his crazed plan.

The best route through the jungle to the shrine leads to each of the locations in turn. If the players decide they want to stray from this sequence, they may do so. However, alternative routes will be more hazardous: roll one die and consult the Jungle Encounter Table.

Alternatively, the players may decide to try to skirt locations – finding alternative routes round them and on to the next location. In this case, you should roll *twice* on the Jungle Encounter Table.

There are yet more menaces in the jungle. To keep up appearances, and to test the adventurers' mettle, the Reaver's mutant Lizard Men will be tracking them. Adventurers will occasionally hear sounds of pursuit from the jungle behind them. Also, whenever they enter a new location or have a Jungle Encounter, roll a die. On a roll of 1, a party of 1–6 mutant Lizard Men will burst from the jungle foliage and attack. Roll each Lizard Man's mutation on the Mutant Lizard Man Table above.

You should be very careful to make Waxley seem convincing. Roll some dice secretly during battles to make it look as if he is fighting. He may even take some wounds. However, it is not necessary for you actually to work out any combats in which he is involved. Waxley is immune to the E.S.P. spell. A wizard who uses the spell will believe Waxley's story to be genuine.

You should do everything you can to make sure that the players do not decide to attack him. Make it quite clear that poor, bedraggled Waxley is their only sure guide through the jungle. He is unarmed (unless one of the adventurers lends him a weapon), and does not look like much of a fighter. If threatened, he will plead for his life, and claim that he will give the adventurers hundreds of Gold Pieces when they take him back to civilization. If the players persist, you should lower each of their LUCK scores by 1 for their foolishness. When he has no further option but to defend himself, the Reaver will reveal his true nature, cast a powerful magic spell which will stun all the adventurers for a minute, and disappear off into the jungle. If they try to follow him, the adventurers will become lost. You will then have to change later episodes as necessary, to allow for Waxley's absence and for the reappearance of the Riddling Reaver at the end of the Act.

Jungle Encounter Table

Die Roll	Encounter
1	1–2 JAGUARS, each SKILL 8, STAMINA 7.
2	2–7 (1 die plus 1) PYGMIES, each SKILL 6, STAMINA 5. If the adventurers have rescued the Pygmies in Location 6, then these will be *Friendly*, and will guide them to the next location – aiding them in battle, if necessary. Otherwise, the Pygmies will be *Unfriendly*.
3	1–2 GREAT APES, each SKILL 8, STAMINA 11, ATTACKS 2.

4	1–6 HEAD-HUNTERS, each SKILL 7, STAMINA 6. If the adventurers have the shaman's mask (Location 4), and display it, the Head-hunters will run away. Otherwise they will attack.
5	Get lost. Roll one die and add one. The adventurers will eventually find their way to this location, after much traipsing through the forest. While the adventurers are lost, roll *twice* to see whether mutant Lizard Men catch them up.
6	1–6 LIZARD MEN, each SKILL 8, STAMINA 8. These are not mutant Lizard Men and are not servants of the Reaver. They hate the Reaver's mutants intensely. If mutants attack the adventurers while they are battling these Lizard Men, then the two types will fight each other and ignore the adventurers!

Further information about the creatures encountered can be found in *Out of the Pit*.

133

134

3

You hack your way through the jungle for an hour or so. You have no way of knowing how far you have travelled, or what direction, but Waxley seems to know where he is going. The trees thin out ahead of you, and as you break through into the open, you see a yawning chasm across your path. Hundreds of feet below, a small stream meanders towards the sea. Looking around for some means of crossing the chasm, you see the two posts of a rope bridge. It is no use now, however, as the rope has been eaten away – obviously by the termites that swarm around the posts.

A little way along the edge you can see a makeshift bridge. A huge, dead, mossy log has been laid across the gap.

The only way to cross the chasm is to walk across the log (the alternative to crossing it is a long trek along its edge, requiring two rolls on the Jungle Encounter Table). Vertigo is not going to be the adventurers' only worry, however, as the bridge is actually the home of a GIANT SPIKE SPIDER. Adventurers who examine the edge of the log carefully will note that it does not seem to be wood – it looks like some kind of resin. Inside this hollow 'log' lurks the Spider. It will wait until its prey reaches the centre of the bridge before striking. A spike will shoot out from inside the log. If an adventurer told you that he was watching the log carefully while crossing, then he may cross safely. If he was not watching the log, he must roll against SKILL to dodge the poisoned spike. If he does not avoid it, he will be paralysed by the Spider's venom, quickly entangled by its webbing, and left suspended from the centre of the log. The Spider will scurry back into its lair to await its next victim.

If they wish to cross safely, or rescue a captured comrade, the adventurers will have to kill the Spider. A player must first avoid the spike, then have one round of combat. If he wins the round, he has successfully lopped off the Spider's spike. If he loses the round, he should *Test for Luck*. If he is Lucky, he has avoided the Spider's sting. If he is Unlucky, he will lose only 1 point of STAMINA, as the paralysing poison is exhausted after the first sting.

Even if the Spider's spike is chopped off, it will still be a menace. The Spider itself will crawl out of its home to fight.

GIANT SPIKE   SKILL 7   STAMINA 6   ATTACKS 2
SPIDER

Should an adventurer attempt to use fire to fight the Spider, he will find it very effective. The 'log' will erupt into flame, and the Spider will be burned up very rapidly. The burning bridge will fall into the chasm, taking any of the Spider's bound victims to their deaths.

Although the adventurers probably will not fall into the chasm, you should add drama by pointing out how far it is to the ground if they fall.

4

Pressing on into the jungle, you find the ground rising. You can see a rocky scarp rising above the trees ahead of you. Finally, you come out of the trees and see an unscalable rock wall. Directly ahead, carved from the rock, is a face. It is no human face – such bloated, malignant features can only be those of some primitive god.

As you approach, you realize just how big the face is. Its gaping mouth is large enough for a Mammoth to lumber into. Its eyes too are huge, and seem to stare at you as if the stone face were alive.

Moving closer, you come across a grisly boundary. Shrunken heads have been laid in a crude semicircle around the face. Some have been picked clean – bare skulls gleaming white. Others are more recent.

If the adventurers stop at the line of skulls, Waxley Speed will explain that according to the map, there is a passage through the rock scarp. There was no mention of the face, but he is very much afraid that the way lies through the mouth of the ancient god.

As soon as someone steps across the line of shrunken heads, a low moaning sound is heard. To their horror, the adventurers will find that it is the heads which are moaning. Read the following to the players:

The moaning of the heads gets louder, and smoke starts to billow from the mouth of the stone god. The feeling that you are being watched is confirmed when you see that the eyes of the stone face are moving! The eyeballs pop out of their stone sockets, and come floating down towards you.

The occupants of the eye-caves are EYE STIN-GERS, guardians of the stone face. The adventurers must fight them. Each of the two Eye Stingers has the following attributes:

EYE STINGER   SKILL 7   STAMINA 2

Eye Stingers resemble huge eyeballs covered in spines, and float about a metre off the ground. Each opponent of an Eye Stinger must *Test for Luck* or be entranced by its hypnotic gaze. Hypnotized victims will be impaled on its spines tipped with a paralysing poison. The paralysis lasts for twenty minutes.

The creatures are very fragile, and filled with a sticky corrosive liquid. When its STAMINA is reduced to zero or below, a Stinger will burst, splattering anyone fighting it with the liquid, which causes 2 points of damage.

The smoke billowing from the mouth of the cave is not of supernatural origin. It comes from a fire lit by the SHAMAN who lives there. The first adventurer to enter the cave will find himself gazing at a huge tribal mask, worn by the head-hunter shaman. Its eyes will glow red, and the adventurer will find himself compelled to turn and fight his nearest comrade! The shaman may control only one adventurer at a time, so the others have a chance to deal with him before their friends kill each other.

SHAMAN   STAMINA 7   SKILL 6

If the shaman is defeated, the adventurers may take his mask, and the crude jewellery which he wears. The jewellery is worth 5 Gold Pieces. The mask requires the primitive magic of the medicine-man to control an opponent, so the adventurers will not be able to make use of its power themselves.

At the rear of the cave, a dank tunnel leads off into the rock. The adventurers will need some form of light. The tunnel's only occupants are a flock of COMMON BATS, which will attack if disturbed by passing adventurers who are noisy (if the players are talking at all after you tell them about the tunnel, then you can assume their characters are also being noisy). Treat the flock of Bats as one opponent. If their STAMINA is reduced to zero, this means that the flock has flown off.

FLOCK OF BATS   SKILL 4   STAMINA 4

On the walls of the tunnel grow some large green mushrooms. If these are eaten they will restore 1–6 points of STAMINA. The effect only happens once, no matter how many mushrooms are eaten. The adventurers may collect as many mushrooms as they wish, but as they lose their healing potency five minutes after being picked, they will be little use in later encounters.

The tunnel finally opens out on the other side of the scarp. Ahead of them the adventurers will see yet more jungle.

You have been travelling for a while, and you are hot and tired. When you come upon a clearing, Waxley suggests a rest. As you slump down on the ground, he idles over to look at the plant in the middle of the clearing. The plant has no branches, and looks lonely in the open space.

You rest your tired limbs for a few minutes, lulled into half-sleep by the heat and the monotonous jungle noises.

Suddenly there is a yell. You leap up, to see a tendril wrapped around Waxley. A hole opens at the foot of the plant and he is dropped into it. There is a despairing wail, abruptly muffled as the pit closes up.

The adventurers must rescue Waxley from the GIANT PITCHER-PLANT, if they are to reach their goal. This plant has submerged its vase in the soft soil to disguise its deadly nature.

PITCHER-PLANT   SKILL 8   STAMINA 7
  TENDRIL

If the tendril wins an attack, it will wrap itself around the adventurer. If it is not defeated in the very next round, that adventurer will be dropped into the pit (the Pitcher-plant's vase) to join Waxley. Characters in the pit will lose 1 point of STAMINA every minute, as they are slowly digested by the plant! They may try to climb out, but the sharp spines on the inside will do them 15 points of damage.

If the tendril is destroyed, it is easy to destroy the vase. Characters may then be safely pulled out. Waxley will be barely alive when rescued, and you should make it clear to the players that he needs some help – magical healing, or at worst a unit of Provisions – to recover his strength. Though they will not realize it until later, the players will be saving the life of the very man they are trying to bring to justice!

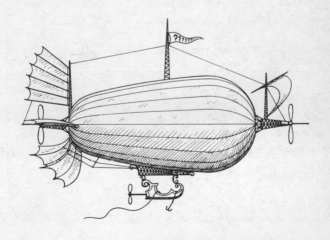

6

*Your journey continues, and you begin to hear a faint
drumming noise from up ahead. As you get nearer, you
also catch the sound of chanting. Some native ritual must
be taking place.*

Ahead of them, a band of HEAD-HUNTERS
have captured two Pygmies. While searching for
magical Yokka Eggs, the Pygmies strayed into carefully laid rope-traps, and are now dangling upside
down, suspended by their tiny feet from a tree. The
Head-hunters are taunting them, and celebrating
their victory over two of their tribe's traditional
enemies. Later, they are planning to make a succulent feast of the little men.

The adventurers will be able to creep up quite
closely, if they successfully move silently (see *Fighting Fantasy*, page 61). They will see twelve extremely
fierce natives, dancing, chanting, and occasionally
poking the Pygmies with their barbed spears. If the
adventurers encountered the shaman, then they
will notice that these Head-hunters have war-paint
in a design similar to the shaman's mask. Each
Head-hunter has the following attributes:

HEAD-HUNTER   SKILL 7   STAMINA 6

Despite their frightening war-paint, the Head-
hunters are not especially brave. If half of their
number are killed, the rest will run away.

If anyone is quick-witted enough to attack them
while wearing the tribal mask of the shaman, they
will all turn tail and flee screaming into the jungle!

The adventurers may decide to free the Pygmy tribesmen. If they do, the short savages will express their gratitude. By way of thanks they will offer a gift – the three Yokka Eggs that they had discovered at the base of the tree.

Yokka Eggs are laid by the mysterious Yokka bird, a fabulously rare creature unique to the area. In the Pygmy tongue, 'yokka' means 'sun', and it is said that the birds fly down from the sun to the earth, to lay their eggs where it is cool. Whether or not this is true, what hatches from a Yokka Egg resembles a ball of fire more than it does a bird. If an egg is broken (for example, by throwing it to the ground), a ball of fire will leap from it, and shoot up into the sky. Anyone caught in the blast will lose 1–6 points of STAMINA. To throw a Yokka Egg accurately, players must roll under their character's SKILL score on two dice. The Eggs are warm to the touch, so the adventurers may decide to keep them to stay warm on cold nights up north!

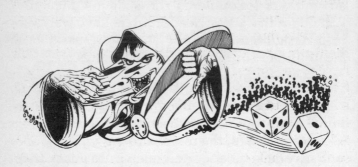

7

The trees thin out once more, and ahead of you lies a stretch of mud-flats. The mud has hardened and cracked, and looks easy to walk across. You should make much faster progress across here. As you are standing in the shade of the trees at the edge of the jungle you notice that tied to a branch of a nearby tree are a number of stiff leathery leaves, about a metre long. Looking closer, you find they are made from several palm leaves, which have been interwoven and stitched together.

The layer of dried mud is quite thin and brittle. Beneath it is quicksand! Anyone who tries to cross the mud-flats without taking precautions will not get very far before the surface cracks beneath his feet. A gout of mud will spurt up, and he will sink into the quicksand. As the wet mud soaks the surface around the break, the surrounding area will turn into sludge, making rescue difficult. Anyone immersed in the quicksand will be sucked down and will disappear completely in five minutes. Comrades must rescue them within this time to save them from a squelchy death. To do this, they will have to use ropes (or, if they have no ropes, creepers from the jungle will do). All that is required to pull someone out is that *one* adventurer makes a successful roll against SKILL (less than SKILL on two dice). All adventurers who are not sinking in the quicksand may make an attempt. If all fail, they may have another go after three minutes.

A short time after the mud is breached, the swamp begins to bubble, a foul-smelling gas taints the air, and the forms of two loathsome MARSH WRAITHS (each SKILL 7, STAMINA 5) begin to take shape. Once formed, they will stand motionless, moaning plaintively. One will talk to the adventurers in his ghostly voice, telling them not to encroach upon the Marsh Wraiths' home.

If the adventurers are to cross the marsh, they must defeat the Marsh Wraiths. However, if they step out on to the mud, they risk being sucked under by the quicksand. The only safe way to cross the mud is to wear the swamp-shoes that were hanging on the tree. These useful objects are used by the Head-hunters to cross the mud-flats without breaking the crust. They work in much the same way as snow-shoes by distributing the wearer's weight over a larger area.

Anyone trying to fight while wearing swamp-shoes will do so at a penalty of −1 to SKILL. If Yokka Eggs are thrown at the Wraiths, then the highly flammable marsh gas will ignite – obliterating the Wraiths, but making the mud-flats an impassable field of fire.

Remember, if the adventurers decide to try to avoid crossing the mud-flats by travelling round their edge, they will have to face two Jungle Encounters before reaching the next location.

8

*Exhausted as he is, Waxley Speed is getting excited. You
are nearing your goal! Ahead of you a white marble temple
rises up from a rocky outcropping. When you get nearer,
you realize that entering will not be very easy. The shrine
sits on a high pedestal of rock, which looks almost unclimb-
able, and a gaping chasm lies between you and the
entrance. On either side of the shrine's entrance sit two
forbidding stone statues of large birds of prey.*

The adventurers have reached the shrine in
which the Pendulum of Fate is guarded. Now all
they must do is enter. The bird statues are FLYING
GUARDIANS. If someone tries to climb up the
pedestal, the Flying Guardians will wait until they
are high up the rock-face, animate themselves and
attack. Fighting off the Guardians while climbing
will be impossible – anyone caught on the rock-face
will be knocked off to his death!

The route across to the shrine is a narrow, invisible bridge. It may be seen as a faint shimmering (like that over a hot pavement) by anyone with the eagle tattoo from Act One, or by the wearer of the eyepatch from Act Two. Alternatively, if the players need a clue of some kind, you should tell them that they see a small bird in mid-air. At first this will not seem unusual, but then they will notice that the bird is not beating its wings, but seems to be sitting in mid-air.

Once the adventurers have discovered the invisible bridge, Waxley will fall dramatically to his knees. Exclaiming that he is too tired to go any further, he will beg to be left as a look-out. He says that if he sees the Reaver approaching, he will hurry to warn them. For now, however, he is in no condition for further exertions.

In fact, since he is an agent of the gods, the bridge will not support him. This is why he cannot enter the shrine, and has had to dupe the players into doing his dirty work for him. His last attempt on the shrine was by airship, but was thwarted by the Flying Guardians.

All that is needed to cross the invisible bridge is bravery. Once the adventurers have entered the temple, you should go straight to Scene Two, 'Shrine of Destiny'.

Scene Two: Shrine of Destiny

Task: Get out of the shrine with the Pendulum of Fate!

About the Shrine

This is no ordinary shrine. Inside the white marble there is not (as you might expect) a place of worship. The shrine contains, or rather consists of, a vast Creature, created in the Godtime (and therefore without a name). When they explore the interior of the shrine, the adventurers will actually be wandering around *inside* the Creature. The interior is lit by phosphorescence, so no lanterns are necessary. If at any time the adventurers use fire, the beast will be wracked with convulsions. They will be thrown about violently, suffering a loss of 1 point of STAMINA per minute until the fire is put out. If a Yokka Egg is broken inside the Creature, the fiery Yokka bird will fly around, trying to escape, and drive the Creature into convulsions. After a few minutes, it will find its way out via the lung chamber.

Another thing the players do not know is the true purpose of the shrine. Apart from the fact that it guards the Pendulum of Fate, it is also an elaborate place of sacrifice. While wallowing in the muck that lines the tunnels of the Creature's insides, the adventurers will slowly be attacked by the Creature's digestive juices. They will lose 1 point of STAMINA for every thirty minutes they are inside the shrine. To escape, the adventurers must reach the heart of the beast, at which beats the Pendulum.

The Scene begins with the adventurers arriving at the entrance chamber, Location 1.

154

1

You open the large, weather-beaten doors of the shrine and pass inside. You find yourselves in a small, square chamber lit by hundreds of candles. By the doors is a pile of several hundred more unlit candles. On the wall opposite you can see a large circle of some black, rubbery hide. There is nothing in the room apart from this, and no sound but that of the eerie howling of the wind outside.

In order to enter the Creature, the adventurers must force it to open its mouth (the circle on the wall opposite). Since the beast is vast, poking or prising will have no effect: it simply will not notice them. They must summon the KEEPER OF THE WAY. The adventurers must light a candle to do this, and you should then read the following:

As you light the candle, the air begins to sparkle in front of the circle on the wall. Brilliant flashes of colour leap before your eyes, temporarily blinding you. A rich, warm voice echoes in your mind:

'Greetings, travellers. It pleases me greatly that in times such as these there are yet some prepared to make the sacrifice and join us. Do not linger, for your destiny awaits.'

Your vision returns, and you can see that the circle is pulsing open and shut. You catch a glimpse of a tunnel beyond, which glows with a dull green luminescence.

To continue, the adventurers must overcome their revulsion and pass through the agitated orifice. When it opens, they will be able to see the phosphorescent glow within, and should realize that they will not need to take the candles in. Once they are all through, the mouth will close behind them.

The tunnel they have entered slopes downward. It is the trachea, or gullet, of the Creature, and leads down to its stomach. The adventurers will be forced along the tunnel as it contracts behind them.

2

After a short journey along the slimy, fleshy tract, you are disgorged into a large chamber. Luckily your landing is cushioned by the gunk that lines its floor. As with the tunnel, this chamber is lit by its phosphorescent walls. It is dome-shaped, although its shape is continually shifting. Its walls throb faintly, and occasionally ducts open in the ceiling and more gunk rains down upon you. Your feet are submerged in the muck, and looking around you can see slime-covered and partially submerged shapes. There are several ducts leading out of the chamber, and you can faintly hear strange sounds emanating from them.

Buried in the muck of this chamber are several skeletons of former sacrifices. Most of their equipment has been corroded, but anyone searching (see *Fighting Fantasy*, page 58) among the bones and sludge will come across a scabbarded sword, which is strangely untarnished. The sword is magical, and the name 'Timakron' is carved in runes on the blade. If its name is shouted before battle commences, it will fractionally speed time up for its wielder. When he is fighting, although he will be moving normally, he will be able to perceive his opponent as moving more slowly, and his SKILL score will therefore be increased by 3 for the combat. The sword was originally wielded by a holy warrior, who used it only against evil races. Because of this it will *never* injure humans, but will use its power to prevent a blow being landed.

There are six exits from this chamber, apart from the tunnel in the ceiling from which the players fell.

As with all the passages inside the Creature, they are circular and small, with a thick layer of sludge coating their floors. From each of the exits comes a distinctive sound. As the adventurers examine each exit, you should describe the appropriate sound, and give any additional description you feel necessary.

Exit A: This leads to the lung chamber. You should suck in and breathe out very slowly through clenched teeth to describe the sound coming from the passage. Tell the players that there is a strong draught from this exit.

Exit B: This leads to the iron-digesting chamber. Tell the players that the passage is quiet, but if they listen long enough, they will hear the occasional slapping sound.

Exit C: This leads to the Mucalytic's chamber. There is a monstrous snorting sound coming from it, along with plenty of churning and squelching.

Exit D: This leads to the grinding chamber. A rumbling and hollow knocking wafts down the passage.

Exit E: This leads to the Wrapper's chamber. There is a faint sound, like the beating of leathery wings.

Exit F: This leads to the blood canal, which in turn connects with the heart. The slow pounding of the Creature's heart can be heard from the passage.

Before the adventurers leave this chamber, they will encounter the WATCHER. Each player should attempt to roll under their SKILL on two dice. Any who succeed will see a small, golden globe float out of a backpack (roll a die to determine whose backpack). Otherwise they will simply notice it hovering in the air near them. Attempts to capture or attack the Watcher will fail; it moves so fast that even Timakron cannot hit it. It will follow everywhere they go in the shrine. The Watcher is one of the Riddling Reaver's devices, being the only way he can see what happens inside the shrine. In his guise of Waxley Speed he had slipped the globe into one of the adventurers' packs before they crossed the invisible bridge. It costs him dearly, in terms of energy, to maintain its flight and speed, but he can use it to help his unknowing pawns in a dire emergency. If you consider the adventurers to be in deadly peril, the Watcher will be able to give aid – but only once. Inside the globe lies a Genie. Its powers are limited within the shrine, but it can bring *one* character back from the dead, or distract an enemy long enough for the adventurers to escape.

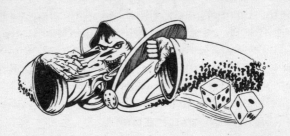

As you edge your way down the tunnel, the draught gets stronger. You feel yourself regularly sucked forward, then pushed back, by the force of the wind. After a short trudge, the tunnel opens out into a large domed chamber. High above you, sunlight streams through a grille. Around the grille are a host of stalactites, making it a very prickly ceiling.

The floor of the chamber rises and falls, and you realize that the wind is produced as air is sucked in and out through the grille. The up-draught is extremely powerful, and you feel the drag pulling at you as the air gushes upwards. If you were to go further into the chamber, you would no doubt be carried up into the air.

If the adventurers look more closely at the ceiling of the chamber, they will see gold glinting among the stalactites close to the grille (a character with the eagle tattoo from Act One will be able to make out a golden chalice). The chalice was carried up there by the draught, and is wedged quite tightly.

Adventurers may decide to try to retrieve it. To do this they will have to find a way of safely riding the up-draught. Getting up is easy: all they have to do is wait until the up-draught begins and step out into the middle of the chamber. They should then *Test for Luck*. If they are Lucky, then they have grasped a stalactite, and will be able to hang on when the down-draught comes. If they are Unlucky, then they have been thrown against the point of a stalactite. They will be able to hold on, but the injury will cost them 3 points of STAMINA.

Once among the stalactites, an adventurer will be able to edge towards the chalice. This is not quite the treasure it may seem – it is actually a SENTINEL. As soon as it is touched, it will transform into a deadly golden warrior. This will fall to the floor (losing 2 points of STAMINA in the process) and attack the other adventurers. Its attributes, after landing on the floor, are as follows:

METAL SENTINEL   SKILL 12   STAMINA 10

The Sentinel cannot be harmed by non-magical weapons, *unless* its opponent is in contact with some gold (holding a Gold Piece would be sufficient).

Once defeated, the Sentinel will transmute back into the form of the golden chalice (which is worth 20 Gold Pieces).

An adventurer up in the stalactites must edge himself away from the column of air to get down: if he waits until there is an up-draught, then lets go, he will drop to the floor quite gently, buoyed up by the weaker up-draught around the edge of the room. You should use your judgement to decide how successful any other methods for getting down will be.

The chamber is twenty metres high. The grille at the top is too fine for an adventurer to squeeze through, and is too securely fixed in place to be removed.

This chamber is suspiciously quiet. Its floor is covered with thick purple hairs, which sprout from pores, like hairs on a turkey-skin. They wave gently in the slight breeze.

The iron-digesting chamber dissolves most of the iron that accumulates in the Creature's innards. The hairs secure whatever it is that is carrying the iron, so that the IRON-EATERS on the ceiling can drop, and begin their work of digesting the items. These will later be passed into the bloodstream of the Creature, to nourish it.

If the adventurers step into the chamber, they will be seized by the Purple Hair.

PURPLE HAIR   SKILL 7   STAMINA 0   (see below)

Play one Attack Round. If the hair wins, then the adventurer has been caught, and an Iron-Eater will drop on him. If the adventurer wins, he has got free from the 'grass' and may escape. In order to break free, an adventurer need win only one Attack Round.

When an Iron-Eater (SKILL 5, STAMINA 0 (see below)) drops on an adventurer, it will begin to feed on his metal armour. Every time it wins an Attack Round, it will digest another item, and the adventurer will lose 1 point of SKILL. If the adventurer wins an Attack Round, then the Iron-eater has been knocked to the floor. It will then be swept away by the hairs.

There are twelve Iron-Eaters on the ceiling, but they will drop only if their prey is held fast.

This passage is extremely narrow, and even more disgusting than the chamber you have just been wallowing in. It goes on for many metres, winding and twisting, and getting viler as you progress further. It also starts to slope downwards. It gets harder to stay on your feet as the slime builds up. The stench is abominable.

The adventurers are approaching the lair of a MUCALYTIC. This foul beast lives like a parasite inside the Creature, revelling in the slime and waste products of the enormous digestive tract. It helps the Creature, since it reduces anything that enters its chamber to an easily digestible mulch!

As they get closer to the Mucalytic's chamber, the adventurers will be assailed by its stench. If they press on, the poisonous stink will make them lose 2 points of STAMINA. They will also have to contend with the slippery slope down into the chamber. Each foolhardy adventurer should roll two dice. If the result is less than their SKILL, then they have kept on their feet. If they fail, then they will slip over, and slide down the tunnel, right into the lap of the Mucalytic.

Its small chamber is full of muck. All that can be seen of the beast itself is its long snout, poking out of a pile of ooze, rather like a periscope. If anyone is stupid enough to enter its lair, it will attack.

MUCALYTIC SKILL 8 STAMINA 9 ATTACKS 2

If the Mucalytic wins three Attack Rounds in a row, it will have grabbed its opponent, who will be drawn inexorably to its mouth. It will breathe deadly poisonous fumes, which will kill the character instantly. Later, if the Mucalytic is not killed, the adventurer will be slowly transformed into slime!

There is no treasure in the room. If an adventurer is killed here, remember that the Watcher may be able to bring him back from the dead. Alternatively, if all the heroes end up in the Mucalytic's lair, the globe might distract the beast, and give them a chance to escape.

A short tunnel leads to a cavernous chamber, full of large, semi-transparent balls. They are rolling around and jostling with one another. As there is no one and nothing else in the chamber, they must be moving themselves in some way. You cannot make out what is inside them, though whatever it is, must be rushing around furiously, for the balls to lurch about so violently. On the floor of the chamber there is a thick layer of powdered debris – obviously crushed by the relentless churning of these curious balls.

There are fifteen balls in the grinding chamber. Inside each of them is a BALL CENTIPEDE. These large relatives of normal centipedes built tough fibrous spherical cocoons to live in. They can move these while inside by running at high speed. Anyone entering the chamber will be set upon by 1–6 of the Grinding Balls.

GRINDING BALL   SKILL 4   STAMINA 3

When a Grinding Ball is reduced to zero STAMINA, it will split into two jagged halves. Out will scuttle the Ball Centipede to attack.

BALL CENTIPEDE   SKILL 7   STAMINA 4

The broken shells will come in very useful as makeshift boats with which to navigate the Creature's bloodstream (Location 8). One person can fit into each half.

As you advance down the tunnel, the noise ahead of you stops. You soon emerge into a dripping chamber. The luminescence of the wall is weaker here, and you have difficulty making out the contents of the room. You see several bones littering the floor, and the occasional glimmer.

The room has quite a high ceiling. Up on the wall above the entrance clings a WRAPPER, a large, leathery being, like a blanket with fangs and claws. Make sure that you know which adventurer is the first to enter the room. He should *Test for Luck*. If he is Lucky, the Wrapper will hurtle into him, but fail to grapple him successfully. It will then glide up into the darkness of the chamber, and back to its perch. If the adventurer is Unlucky, he will be grabbed, lose 2 STAMINA points, and be enshrouded in its wings. The wrapped adventurer will find it very hard to hit the Wrapper, and must reduce his SKILL by 3. Other adventurers may attack the Wrapper, but they will risk injuring their companion. If they *lose* an Attack Round, they will do 1 point of damage to him!

WRAPPER   SKILL 12   STAMINA 9

If the Wrapper fails in its first attack it will return to its perch until the party *leaves* the chamber. It will then silently swoop on the last person to leave, who should *Test for Luck*, as above.

A number of skeletons are in the Wrapper's lair. Several have some treasure. Adventurers searching the chamber will recover 3–18 Gold Pieces (roll three dice) and 1–6 jewels, each worth 10 Gold Pieces.

As you move down the tunnel, the pounding noise gets louder. Soon the tunnel opens out, and you see a rushing stream ahead of you. In the dull glow of the walls it looks very dark. Moving closer you see that it is red. It must be a river of blood! It gushes past in a raging torrent. Clearly, anyone trying to swim in it will be swept away.

The adventurers have found the bloodstream of the Creature. It is like a subterranean river, flowing round the Creature's body to provide nourishment for its organs. The adventurers must travel down the stream to the heart, if they are to recover the Pendulum of Fate and escape from the shrine.

The current of the stream is very fierce, and anyone trying to swim in it will quickly be swept away and drowned. The only safe way to navigate the stream is to use the shell halves from Location **6** as coracles (small hemispherical boats). The players may need hints to realize this: use Dappa, if he is still around. Paddles will be unnecessary, as the current will sweep them to their goal – all the adventurers need to do is hang on! The stream leads to Location **9**, the heart chamber.

9

You are swept along by the torrent, veering dangerously close to the walls as you swish round bends in the tunnel. Every now and then a fresh stream joins the main branch, and you hang on for grim life in these turbulent waters. By the reddish glow of the stream you can make out stalactites, hanging low over the river like the fangs of a Dragon. You barely manage to avoid these deadly spikes.

After a nightmare journey, the stream empties into a vast cavern. The pounding sound is deafening, and the lake of blood swirls round like a giant whirlpool. At its centre is a small island. In the centre of the island is a pedestal, with two huge immobile figures grappling over it.

The current will carry the adventurers closer and closer to the island. As they approach, they will be able to see the figures more clearly. They are identical in every respect, save their colour – one is black, the other white. They are powerfully muscled, with fists like sledge-hammers. Their heads are blank and featureless. Beneath them, on the pedestal, sits the source of the constant beat that fills the chamber. The Creature's heart is driven by the Pendulum of Fate, which is encased in a short unbreakable glass tube. The Pendulum itself is very small (about ten centimetres long), yet swings very slowly. It will continue to swing no matter what is done to it.

The adventurers will be able to beach their improvised boats on the island and approach the pedestal. As they do so, they will experience powerful emanations from the two figures. The black figure radiates a malign influence of pure Evil, sending shivers down the adventurers' spines, while the white figure counters this with an aura of Goodness. If anyone touches the pedestal or the Pendulum, the two figures will animate, and begin to battle each other, ignoring the adventurers completely. It will soon become obvious that the two are perfectly matched. Each blow landed is returned with equal force, and neither seems to be able to press home an advantage.

If the adventurers intervene in the battle in the slightest way, perhaps siding with the Good figure, then the balance will be upset. Within seconds, that figure will have smashed its opponent into a thousand shards.

The figures are the ICON OF GOOD and the ICON OF EVIL, pure personifications of their essences. Once one is defeated, the remaining Icon will turn to the adventurers and speak. Whichever one remains, it will say virtually the same thing:

'I am the Icon of Good (Evil). I must battle all that is tainted and impure. There is Evil (Good) within you – I can sense its presence. You must be purified.'

Ignore the bracketed words if the white Icon survives. If the black Icon survives, however, you should substitute the words in brackets.

The Icon will then attack.

ICON   SKILL 12   STAMINA 20

If an adventurer removes the Pendulum from the pedestal, the pounding noise will abruptly cease. The whirlpool of blood will slow down and finally stop. The adventurers will be able to make their escape from the Creature quite easily. The blood will drain from the lake and channels in a matter of minutes, and the adventurers will be able to find their way back up the tunnel and into a duct leading to the stomach chamber. The fleshy walls of this will have sagged downwards, and the channel through which they entered will be easily reached. At its top, the Creature's mouth will be hanging open, and the adventurers may crawl out and into the entrance chamber. All the candles will have been snuffed out. You should then go to Ending the Scene.

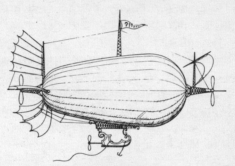

Ending the Scene

The adventurers have succeeded in escaping the Shrine of Destiny with the Pendulum of Fate. However, a little surprise awaits them still. Read out the following:

You stagger out of the temple and across the invisible bridge. You have succeeded! The fresh air has never tasted so sweet, and you gulp down great lungfuls to rid yourself of the foul stench of the enormous Creature's innards.

With elation, you notice that Waxley Speed is still waiting for you. He seems a little changed, however. He is no longer wearing the same tattered garb, but flowing robes. He hails you:

'Greetings, adventurers. I see you've brought me my little trinket. That'll be very useful. You know, Good and Evil will never be the same again.'

As he speaks, the golden globe which followed you through the shrine shoots in front of you. There is a flash, and the next moment the Pendulum has been wrenched from you and is dangling from the globe. The golden sphere floats across to the man you knew as Waxley.

'Thank you,' he continues. 'You've all done very well – I really must congratulate you. But I'm afraid I must be going: I've got an airship to catch!'

As he says this, you are engulfed in the shadow of an enormous flying craft. Waxley, or rather the Riddling Reaver, raises the golden orb above his head with both hands. He floats into the air and enters the flying ship.

You have succeeded in escaping from the shrine, but it seems that victory belongs to your enemy!

This is the end of Act Three, 'The Pendulum of Fate'. The Riddling Reaver has escaped with the artefact to his lair. The final Act, 'The Realm of Entropy', tells of what he intends to do with it.

ACT FOUR
THE REALM OF ENTROPY

Players' Tale

A mighty artefact has been stolen from your grasp! The quizzical villain known as the Riddling Reaver has seized the Pendulum of Fate. This ancient device is said to give power over Good and Evil. Who knows for what perverse ends the Reaver intends to use it?

The villain escaped by means of an enormous flying monstrosity. Your only chance to defeat him is to follow the craft and track him to his lair. You therefore hurry off into the surrounding jungle. The airship is heading for higher rocky ground, which you can see ahead of you. Luckily it is not travelling too fast, and you still have it in sight when it descends. You cannot make out exactly where it has gone, but it went down very close to a large waterfall. You must make your way to the falls and try to find an entrance to the Riddling Reaver's hideout.

As you press on, you notice that something very odd is happening to the jungle plants around you. The further you walk, the stranger their colours get. Very soon you are no longer walking through a green and brown jungle, but one which is a riot of colour, with reds, blues, yellows, oranges and purples in profusion. What is more, the shapes of the plants seem to have changed. The familiar shrubs and trees seem to have been warped out of all recognition – their forms apparently determined purely by Chance. You seem to have strayed into a realm of entropy, where the only law of the universe is Chance.

REAVER'S ROOST

178

GamesMaster's Tale

The Act commences with the adventurers tracking their enemy to his secret hideaway. They stray into the field of Chance which marks his domain, and encounter its effects in the form of a chaotic array of plants. They then discover that the waterfall which they had seen from a distance flows upwards. They realize that it is the only way up, and after watching a party of the Reaver's servants, they throw themselves into the fall, and are carried up and along the river. The river throws them up at a set of marble steps. They have found the entrance to the Riddling Reaver's lair. Exploring the rooms beyond, the adventurers will find that in the Reaver's stronghold Luck and Chance rule, and many impossible things may happen. They must find their way through the menaces of the outer chambers to the Reaver's underground inner sanctum and laboratory.

Finally, the heroes will catch up with the villain as he prepares to use the Pendulum of Fate. His plan is to change the beliefs of people and creatures all the way across Allansia. Suddenly, it will no longer be so easy to decide who is good and who is evil, as so many will have changed. This will lead to many deaths and make it impossible for the Forces of Good and Evil to know how powerful they are. In the confusion, Chance will dominate. There will be a new balance between Good and Evil, and the Trickster Gods of Luck and Chance will rule.

The whole Act happens in the Reaver's domain. The adventurers will start the scenario as they reach the waterfall. You should therefore go to Location 1.

Scene One: The Reaver's Roost

Task: To gain access to the Reaver's inner sanctum.

1

You finally arrive at the waterfall and find your way to a small ledge very close to the torrent. You soon realize that there is something very wrong. Your attention is drawn to a gnarled piece of driftwood that has been caught in the roiling white water. It is carried upwards! The law of gravity has been reversed for this waterfall, as the water is plummeting up from the pool below you, to flow over the edge of the cliff above. As you peer into the falls, you notice another ledge on the opposite side of the falls. You can make out a number of blurred figures, each carrying a large, bulging sack. They seem to be a number of different colours, and there is something strangely insubstantial about them. To your amazement, they hurl themselves off the ledge, and fly up and over the lip of the falls.

The adventurers have spotted a party of the Reaver's REPLICANTHS returning from a scavenging mission. They will encounter them later, and discover the secret of their origin. Meanwhile they must face the problem of reaching the Reaver's lair.

There is no sign of the villain's airship, but it went down somewhere just beyond the falls. The cliffs on either side are sheer, and will be very difficult to climb. You should make it clear to the players that it is very unlikely that their characters would all be able to make it to the top alive.

The Replicanths have shown them the only safe way up, and the adventurers just have to summon up enough courage to follow them.

If they do hurl themselves off the ledge, each player should roll four dice against their STAMINA scores. If they have rolled lower, then they are fine. If they have rolled higher than or equal to their STAMINA, they have swallowed some water while being buffeted in the fall, and lose 1 point of STAMINA. They should have kept their mouths shut!

Once the adventurers have fallen up the falls, go to Location 2.

2

*Travelling the falls is an exhilarating experience. You fly
upwards, your limbs flailing, and water lashes your faces.
You shoot over the top of the falls, and drop with a splash
into the water. The mighty current drags you along for a
little way, then washes you up on the shore. Before you is a
magnificent building. It is built of white marble blocks
with multicoloured veins. Above it floats the huge airship,
moored to a tall pine tree which rises from the roof. The
palace has no windows, but ahead of you a flight of marble
steps lead up to a very impressive pillared entrance. On
the grass near by, a large butterfly is chasing a tiny yellow
Tyrannosaurus, and above you a blackbird flies past
upside down.*

*As soon as you place a foot on the marble steps, a small,
childlike figure materializes in a puff of sparkling colour.
He is wearing a tall hat, a smart green suit and shiny shoes
with large buckles. He ignores you, and concentrates on
juggling three exquisite green glass bottles.*

The juggling figure is Finnegan O'Dinnegan, a LEPRECHAUN. He is juggling three stolen GENIE bottles. If the adventurers approach up the steps, he will tell them that he is in charge of guarding against intruders. But he says he is bored of juggling the bottles and wants a break. If one of the party will take over for a short while, he will see what he can do to get them inside.

If one of the adventurers agrees to take over, Finnegan will toss the bottles in his direction and race up the steps and through the doors. The adventurer who agreed to juggle the bottles must first catch them. This requires a roll under SKILL on two dice. Then he must begin juggling. Initially he must make another roll against SKILL on two dice to succeed. As he continues juggling, however, the bottles feel heavier and heavier, and he must roll against SKILL twice more. If all of these rolls are successful, then Finnegan will return, congratulate him on his dexterity, take back the bottles and point to the now open doors. If the adventurer fails on *any* roll, however, he will have dropped one of the bottles to the ground. You should then read the following:

The bottle falls to the ground and shatters. A thick cloud of purple gas forms above the broken glass, and the form of a Genie takes shape. He seems to sway unsteadily, as if seasick, and he addresses you in a booming, though rather unsteady voice: 'Which way did that rascal Finnegan go? Tell me now or I'll turn you into jellyfish!'

If the adventurers point to the doors, the furious Genie will race through them (leaving them open behind him). If they refuse to tell the Genie where Finnegan went, he will threaten to turn them into jellyfish; if they continue to refuse to tell him, he will carry out his threat!

If the adventurers refuse Finnegan's offer, or if they do not actually juggle the bottles, he will not open the doors and they will find it very difficult to get into the building. The huge doors cannot be forced open, and there is no other way inside. If they wait for ten minutes without acting, then the doors will open, and a scavenging party of five REPLICANTHS will emerge. These peculiar servants of the Reaver come in different shapes, sizes and colours, but have all been created in their master's laboratory. Each looks like a skeleton encased in jelly. Each Replicanth has the following attributes:

REPLICANTH   SKILL 6   STAMINA 4

If the adventurers defeat the Replicanths, they will be able to sneak in through the doors.

3

Passing through the enormous doors, you find yourselves in a long hall. It is carpeted with well-mown grass, and in its centre sits a picturesque wishing-well. There are three ivy-covered doors off the left and the right walls, and one door directly opposite.

If the adventurers encountered the party of Replicanths outside, then ignore the next section, otherwise read it out to the players:

By the door opposite, five colourful creatures are busily at work, tipping the contents of sacks into a hole in the wall. As you enter, they turn and look at you. You see with revulsion that they are human-shaped lumps of jelly, within which the skeleton can clearly be seen. They lumber menacingly towards you.

If the adventurers did not encounter the Replicanths outside, they will have to fight them here. Each of the five Replicanths has the following attributes:

REPLICANTHS   SKILL 6   STAMINA 4

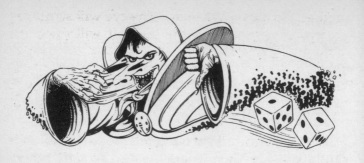

If they have already fought the Replicanths, they may start examining the contents of the hall straight away. The well in its centre is apparently bottomless. If anything is dropped into it, it will quickly fall out of sight. Fifteen seconds later a hole will materialize in the ceiling, the object will drop from it, and the hole will disappear. The object will hit the head of anyone peering down the well. If the object they threw down is quite hard (such as a coin), it will do them 1 point of injury. If it is larger, it will actually knock them down the well. They will disappear downwards, only to reappear seconds later out of the mysterious hole in the ceiling. They will fall indefinitely until rescued.

Players may wish for whatever they like after throwing something down the well. Whatever it is, they will not get it!

Light in the hall (as in most of the rest of the building) is provided by a glowing ceiling.

The six doors off the long walls have handles, and can easily be opened. The one in the far wall is large and metallic. It has no handle, but set into its centre is a large eye. Beneath this is a hastily scrawled notice: 'Go away, I'm busy.' The eye will scrutinize everyone approaching the door. It will open the door only if it sees the Riddling Reaver's face (or its likeness – one of the stuffed Reavers of later locations will do fine!). Otherwise the door will squawk, 'You're not my master, you're not coming through!'

To one side of the door is a hatch in the wall, labelled 'Bones'. The hatch opens easily, revealing a chute leading down into darkness. This is where the Replicanths deposit the bones which they collect for the Reaver to manufacture more of their kind. A player may slide down the chute if he wishes, but will lose a point of STAMINA from the painful landing on the pile of bones. Read out the description of Location 4 of Scene Two to them (page 219). Players will not be able to leave that chamber by the door, as it is barred from the outside: they will have to climb back up the chute.

Each time the adventurers return to the hall, they risk encountering one of its denizens. Roll on the Hall Encounter Table. Moreover, each time they return the sign on the eye-door will be different. You should decide what it says, along the lines of 'Buzz off, I'm working'; 'I told you to go away'; 'I'm warning you – leave me alone!'

Hall Encounter Table

Roll one die and consult the table. Encounters 4–6 can only happen once each. Once you have had one of these, subtract three from the number if you roll it again. For example, once the characters have met Finnegan, if you roll 4 it will count as 1, and the adventurers will have no encounter.

Die Roll	Encounter
1	No encounter.
2	A party of 1–6 Replicanths (each SKILL 6, STAMINA 4) enter the hall. Roll a die. If the result is *even*, they will enter from the main doors, each carrying a sack of bones to deposit in the bones chute. If the result is *odd*, they will come out of the eye-door, shutting it behind them.
3	The door across the hall from the adventurers will open. The Riddling Reaver will pop his head round it, thumb his nose at them, blow a raspberry at them, then slip back into the room, slamming the door shut behind him. This is actually a repeating Illusion spell the Reaver once cast as a tease.
4	Finnegan the Leprechaun will pop up out of nowhere. His reaction to the adventurers will depend on whether or not they juggled his bottles. If a bottle was broken, he will hurl insults at the person who broke it and show the

bruises that the Genie dealt him. He will
tell the character, 'You're all thumbs,'
and disappear. The adventurer will then
discover that all his fingers have been
turned into thumbs! His SKILL will be
reduced by 3 until the curse wears off
(half an hour).

If the character juggled the bottles
successfully, Finnegan will give him a
five-leafed clover, which will increase the
character's LUCK score by 4 for as long as
he has it.

If the characters ignored Finnegan, he
will float past, nose in the air,
nonchalantly juggling three bottles with
one hand. He will disappear, and a few
seconds later there will be a shattering
sound, closely followed by yelps of pain.
As the adventurers enter the hall, they
see one of the most utterly revolting
creatures they have ever clapped eyes
on, sitting on the edge of the well. Words
cannot do full justice to its fearsome
appearance, but its leathery wings, huge
slavering jaws, repulsive scaly hide and

5

hulking frame would reduce hardened monster-killers to quivering jelly. If the players stay in the hall, rather than cowering back into the room they have just been in, it will turn and face them. If they thought its side view was bad, the full frontal is appalling! It is a TREMLOW, perhaps the most fearsome-looking beast in Allansia – but also the most cowardly (which is why so few are seen!). Taking one look at the adventurers, it will shriek in horror, throw its distended arms into the air, and bolt for the door, whining pitifully. The adventurers will not be able to catch it before it flies off to safer haunts.

6 The adventurers will notice a buzzing sound as they enter the hall. A little old man is shuffling up and down the hall, holding a GIANT DRAGONFLY (SKILL 8, STAMINA 4) on a lead. The Dragonfly hovers a few centimetres off the ground, and seems to be cropping the grass with its mandibles. The old man mows his way up to the adventurers without noticing them, and then looks up, startled. As he does so, the Dragonfly tears the lead out of his hand. It will fly twice round the hall at breakneck speed before swooping to attack the adventurers. The old man will flee out of the hall.

1

Just before the adventurers open the door to this 'room', you should roll one die and add 4: the room with that number is the room they enter when the door is opened. The door is a transporting door. Once the adventurers have shut it behind them they will not be able to pass back through into Location 5. If the players tell you their characters are holding the door open, they will be able to go back into the Stuffed Adventurers' Room. It is perfectly possible for the door to transport them into Location 5 – if this is the case they will be able to look around and see themselves entering!

You should roll for a new location each time the door of transportation is opened.

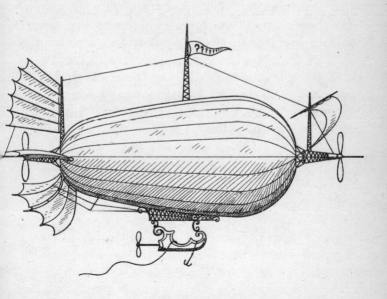

Inside is a long room. Its walls, ceilings and floor are all bare wooden boards. A group of figures stand motionless near you, facing the opposite wall, on which there is a door. They seem strangely familiar, but you cannot make out their features.

The occupants of this room are stuffed replicas of the adventurers! They stand together in a little group, frozen in the act of walking across the room. No matter what the adventurers do to them, they will not animate. Their only unusual property is that they will play an odd game of 'Grandmother's Steps'. If the adventurers decide to walk across the room to the far door, halfway across they will feel the urge to look round. They will see no movement, but their stuffed duplicates will have moved several metres towards them. This will continue to happen as they make their way further across the room.

If the players tell you that their characters are watching the stuffed figures as they walk to the door, they will see nothing. The stuffed figures can never be caught in the act of moving.

6

The room is obviously a library. Shelves of books line the walls, and opposite you there is a reading-desk. At the desk, facing away from you, sits a robed figure, intent on the book before him. It seems you have cornered your quarry!

The figure at the desk looks exactly like the Riddling Reaver, even down to his robe. But the players should know some of their opponent's quirks by now! It is a stuffed replica of the Reaver which sits studying the book. The whimsical schemer likes to have a stuffed version of himself sitting in here, as he feels it gives the place a 'friendlier atmosphere'.

Whatever the adventurers do, the figure will not move. If they attack it, they will easily chop it into pieces. The Reaver stuffed it with stinging Flies, however, and when released these will attack everyone in the room. Adventurers must beat a hasty retreat from the room to avoid losing 1 point of STAMINA for every thirty seconds they remain in it. The only effective weapon against the Flies is fire. If the adventurers find a way of attacking the Flies

with fire, then you should treat the whole swarm as one creature to be fought:

SWARM OF FLIES   SKILL 6   STAMINA 4

The book which the stuffed Reaver is examining is made up entirely of blank pages. If the adventurers examine any of the other books in the room they will find that these also have blank pages, but they will also discover the reason for this – the books are talking books! As soon as a book is opened, it will begin to talk. It will describe its subject, or tell a story. The book will continue talking until either it is shut or someone shouts 'STOP!' at it. If a shut book is opened it will always begin at the beginning. If an adventurer shouts 'START!' at a book which had been stopped, it will carry on where it left off.

The Reaver's book-collection is quite varied, with a good selection of history, legends and folk-tales. One of the first books the adventurers will come across is titled *Teach Yourself Demon-summoning*, by Jaiphrai Ah'cha. As soon as it is opened it will begin to explain the ritual for summoning a FIRE DE-MON. If the adventurers allow it to continue to its end, the ritual will be completed, and the Demon will be summoned. It will attack immediately.

FIRE DEMON   SKILL 10   STAMINA 10   ATTACKS 3

The Fire Demon will shoot gouts of fire from its fiery nostrils. These hit on a roll of 1–4 on one die, doing 2 points of extra injury, whether it has won or lost the Attack Round. If the Fire Demon is killed, it will be engulfed in its own flames and disappear.

7

You have found the Riddling Reaver's dining-room. A long and impressive table runs the length of the room, laden with a succulent feast. Guests line the table, though instead of sitting on chairs they seem to be floating in huge bottles. At the head of the table opposite you sits the Riddling Reaver. He stares glumly at you.

The Reaver's dining-room reflects his macabre sense of humour. His guests are all former enemies whom he has preserved in large pickling-jars. The figure at the head of the table is not the Riddling Reaver himself, but one of his stuffed duplicates. It will not speak, but it has been animated so that it can fight. If the adventurers disturb the feast on the table (the food is excellent, by the way), it will stand up, draw a barbed scimitar and attack. Whatever happens, it will preserve the same glum expression on its face.

STUFFED RIDDLING   SKILL 8   STAMINA 6
  REAVER

When the stuffed Reaver is cut open (when it is reduced to zero STAMINA), its contents will spill out. It is filled with a thick paste, which expands on contact with air, rather like rising dough. After expanding it will set solid. Anyone remaining in the room will be caught in the sticky paste when it expands. They must be pulled out by friends (two people must make successful rolls against SKILL), otherwise they will be encased when it solidifies.

8

This chamber is exceedingly plush. Gorgeous tapestries hang from the walls, the floor is richly carpeted, and exotic couches are covered with cushions. In one reclines a familiar robed figure. The Riddling Reaver seems to be relaxing, heedless of your presence. Over on the wall to your left is a rack of bottles, from which you can hear a faint tapping.

This is the Reaver's sitting-room, where he comes to relax from the busy life of being an agent of the gods. As with the library, he keeps a stuffed replica of himself in here to give the room a friendlier feel. This is not animated, but is stuffed with small downy feathers. Anyone attacking the recumbent figure will cut it open very easily, only to be engulfed in a swirling mass of feathers. They should *Test for Luck.* If they are Unlucky, they will sneeze uncontrollably for the next ten minutes, lose 1 point of STAMINA, and fight at – 2 to SKILL.

At first glance, the rack of bottles appears to be the Reaver's wine-collection. In fact only two of the nine bottles contain wine. The others act as the Reaver's dungeons! The tapping sound is caused by one of the inmates. If the adventurers examine the bottle, they will see the tiny figure of a woman inside. Pulling the cork on the bottle frees her. A cloud of gas will swirl out, and she will coalesce out of it. She is short and dark, with a mischievous glint in her eyes. Her clothes are practical, and she carries a shortsword. She introduces herself to the adventurers as Baba Lai and thanks them profusely for rescuing her. She explains that she is the leader of a band of adventurers who set out to rid the world of the menace of the Riddling Reaver. Unfortunately, they were caught by a Genie, who imprisoned them in the bottles. She begs the adventurers to free her six comrades by uncorking the other bottles.

If they release all her companions, however, they will discover that Baba Lai was not being entirely honest. In fact, she and her friends were caught looting by the Reaver's Genie. They are out for any money and treasure they can get their hands on – and this will include that of the adventurers! Once they are all freed, they will attack.

	SKILL	STAMINA
BABA LAI	8	15
CUT-THROAT	6	12

The robber band will not all fight to the death. If three of them are killed, or if Baba herself is defeated, the remainder will cut and run.

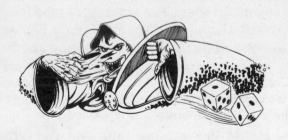

9

You have entered a long hall, tiled with a chequered black and white pattern. Leading off the hall are a number of small doors, like cupboards. Each of these seems to have writing on it.

The doors in this hall lead to Riddle Cupboards. Each has a riddle written on it, which describes its contents. Adventurers may discover the contents of the cupboards either by solving the riddles, or by opening the doors. It is a lot riskier to open the doors without having some idea of what is inside, however, as the adventurers will soon find out.

There are eight cupboards, four on each side of the hall. Running down the left-hand wall are cupboards A–D, while E–H are on the right. As the adventurers examine each door, you should read out the riddle which corresponds to it, so that the players can copy it down.

Cupboard A
In a corner on the wall
I lie in wait for my prey.
Without fists or polearms
I stretch my nets around me;
And my table is seldom bare.

Inside the cupboard is a GIANT SPIDER. It will attack anyone opening its cupboard.

GIANT SPIDER SKILL 7   STAMINA 8   ATTACKS 2

Cupboard B

I've seen you where you never was
And where you ne'er will be;
And yet you in that very same place
May still be seen by me.

Adventurers opening the cupboard door will see an image of themselves, reflected in a mirror.

Cupboard C

Long legs, crooked toes,
Glassy eyes, snotty nose.

The cupboard contains a GIANT FROG (SKILL 5, STAMINA 7). If its door is opened, it will spring out, propelled by its powerful hind legs. It will not fight unless attacked, but will hop around the room quite violently. Whenever the adventurers are in this room when the Frog is loose, they must say that they are keeping an eye on it. If they do not, then one of them (roll a die to find which one) will be knocked sprawling by it. If the adventurers are in combat and the Frog is free, it will knock someone over every other Attack Round. Anyone knocked over must spend a round getting up, during which he may not fight – so an opponent will score a free blow on him, unless someone steps in to help.

Cupboard D

What has a thousand legs and can't walk?

Crammed into this cupboard are five hundred pairs of breeches. Anyone opening the door will be buried beneath a large pile of cloth!

Cupboard E

I have a little house which I live in all alone,
Without doors, without windows,
And if I want to go out I have to break through the
  wall.

The cupboard contains a single Yokka Egg (see page **146** for details), sitting on a velvet cushion.

Cupboard F

He who has it doesn't tell it;
He who takes it doesn't know it;
He who knows it doesn't want it.

Inside the cupboard is a large pile of Gold Pieces. Since there are 300, it would seem to be a major haul, but the coins are actually counterfeit, made from a cheap alloy with a thin coating of gold. An adventurer who examines the coins carefully, and scratches one of them, will remove the coating and discover the truth. If the adventurers decide to take the 'treasure', they may have to leave other items behind, since 300 Gold Pieces weigh a lot. You should use your judgement to decide whether their load is too heavy.

Cupboard G

I haunt, all pale, the waters of foul fens;
Fortune has fashioned me a bloody name,
For greedy gulps of red blood are my fare.
No bones, or feet, or arms at all have I,
Yet bite with three-forked wounds unlucky men,
And by health-bringing lips thus conquer care.

As soon as this door is opened, a flood of water will gush forth, completely drenching the adventurer who opened it. And there is worse: in the water are five large LEECHES, which will latch on to the adventurer who opened the door, and will begin to suck blood. If they are not removed, the character will lose 1 point of STAMINA per minute from the effects of the Leeches. However, removing them is a nasty business. Pulling off a Leech rips a wound in the adventurer – causing loss of 2 points of STAMINA. So pulling off all five leeches would cost the unlucky character 10 STAMINA points.

The safest way to remove Leeches is to force them to release their grip by burning them off. If the adventurers can find some way of holding the Leeches very close to fire *without* harming the adventurer (for example, by using the wick of a lantern), all will be fine. If they try something unsubtle, like burning a Leech off with a flaming brand, the adventurer will lose 1 point of STAMINA each time.

Cupboard H

We are little Brethren twain,
Arbiters of Loss and Gain.
Many to our Counters run,
Some are made, and some undone.
But, as Men find to their Cost,
Few are made, but Numbers lost.
Though we play them Tricks for ever,
Yet they always want our Favour.

Sitting on a satin cushion inside the cupboard are two small ivory dice. These are the Dice of Logaan, and are powerful magical items. Any time a player is not in combat, he may elect to roll the Dice of Logaan. Take a pair of dice and nominate one as plus, one as minus. Roll the pair, and subtract the result of the minus die from that of the plus. Apply the final result to the character's LUCK score (for example, if the minus die is 4 and the plus die is 3, then the character would lose 1 point of LUCK).

Alternatively, the dice may be used as a last-ditch measure in combat. If the adventurers are doing battle, they may do down their opponents by means of the dice. Take a pair of dice and nominate one as the SKILL die, the other as the STAMINA die. Roll the dice and note the results. You should then take the value of the SKILL die off the opponent's SKILL, and the value of the STAMINA die off the opponent's STAMINA. If the adventurers are fighting more than one opponent, you should tell them the results, and let them divide the penalties among their opponents as they see fit. Throwing the dice in this manner can only be done once – the dice will then lose their magical powers.

A strange sight greets your eyes as you enter this room. Three weird disc-shaped creatures seem to be torturing a poor fellow. They have bound him hand and foot, and as you watch, two of them hurl him into the air. The other shouts 'Heads!' as they do so. The man lands painfully on his knees, and the two throwers raise a cheer. Some Gold Pieces are slid across the floor, and you notice that there are two piles of gold and silver. Then the creatures notice you. They frown at you and wait expectantly.

The round creatures are WHEELIES. The adventurers have interrupted their gambling game. If the adventurers approach them in a friendly manner, they will explain the game, and will let them play for a while.

The game is quite simple. First of all, wagers are laid. Then two of the Wheelies throw the bound prisoner into the air, and the remaining one shouts 'Heads' or 'Tails'. Depending on which part of his body the prisoner lands on, the bet is won or lost – winner takes all.

If the adventurers agree to play, the Wheelies will team up against them. All three will throw the prisoner into the air, and the adventurers must choose 'Heads' or 'Tails'. One of the adventurers should be nominated as the spokesman, who will make the call. The players should decide who does this. Then play out a number of rounds. The game can continue for as long as each side still has some money to gamble, and the adventurers still want to carry on. Run each round as follows:

1. Decide how much money is to be wagered on the throw. The money must be shown: adventurers cannot bet money they do not have. The Wheelies will match the bet if they can, otherwise they will bet as much as they have.
2. The Wheelies will then toss the prisoner into the air. The adventurers' spokesman must call 'Heads' or 'Tails'.
3. Roll a die. If the result is 1–3, the prisoner has landed on his head, arms or upper body (this counts as 'Heads'); if the result is 4–6, he has landed on his legs or lower body (this counts as 'Tails').
4. If the adventurers guessed correctly, then they get their bet back, along with that of the Wheelies. If they guessed wrong, then they lose their bet. Go back to 1 and start again.

The Wheelies have 57 Gold Pieces and 64 Silver Pieces with which to bet (10 Silver Pieces = 1 Gold Piece).

If the adventurers do not seem interested in the game, take a dislike to the Wheelies, or want to rescue the prisoner, they will have to fight them. Before battle is joined, the Wheelies will have a chance to spin round, each throwing one of their knives at the adventurers. These hit on a roll of 1–3, doing 2 points of STAMINA damage. Each of the three Wheelies has the following attributes:

WHEELIE   SKILL 7   STAMINA 6

The prisoner, unfortunately, has been driven mad by his ordeal. He can do nothing except babble numbers, and will show no gratitude if rescued and freed from his bonds. He will sink down into a corner, talking to himself, and refuse to budge from it.

Ending the Scene

The Scene ends when the adventurers find the means to get through the eye-door. All they have to do is ensure that the eye sees the Reaver's face. There are three stuffed Reavers in this Scene, and of these, two can easily be dragged out of their rooms and shown to the eye. Alternatively, if one of the adventurers is a wizard, an illusion of the Reaver would do fine.

When the adventurers pass through the eye-door, they will see a flight of stairs ahead of them. These lead down into the Reaver's laboratory. You should now proceed to Location 1 of the final Scene, 'In the Laboratory'.

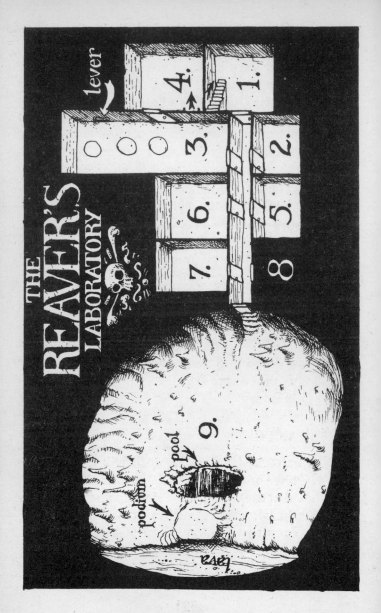

THE REAVER'S LABORATORY

Scene Two: in the Laboratory

Tasks: Defeat the Reaver! Escape the laboratory.

1

You edge your way down the stairs, noticing that the light has changed colour. The ceiling is now glowing an eerie shade of blue. Coming to the bottom, you find yourself in a small empty room. There is a door in the opposite wall of the room. You can dimly hear a strange rumbling noise, but you cannot tell exactly where it is coming from.

This room is the entrance to the Reaver's laboratory. It is completely empty. The door is unlocked. If the players open it, they will see a corridor leading into the blue gloom. There are doors on either side of the corridor. The corridor leads to the various rooms within which the Reaver performs his experiments. Every five minutes, a Replicanth will come out of the first door on the right (Room 3), and make its way along the corridor to the room at the end, which it will enter. If the adventurers are in the corridor they will have to fight the Replicanth.

REPLICANTH   SKILL 6   STAMINA 4

When attacked, the Replicanth will try to *Escape* (see *Fighting Fantasy*, page 54). You should work out which end of the corridor the Replicanth will be able to escape to. If it reaches the Production Room (Room 3), it will return with five of the eight Replicanths from that room. If it reaches the Reaver's Sanctum (Room 9), it will return with 2–12 of its fellows.

2

This room is wood-panelled, and has shelves all the way around the wall, on which sit racks of test-tubes. The test-tubes are all stoppered and labelled, and contain powders of different colours. At one end of the room is a trough full of water. As you opened the door, you created a draught, and this has blown a stack of papers into one of the test-tube racks. A test-tube of icy blue powder is knocked out, rolls gently along the shelf, then falls down on to the water trough. The glass shatters, and a faint sprinkling of the powder settles on the water. There is a furious bubbling, which slowly dies down. Then you notice a pair of beady eyes watching you from over the edge of the water trough.

This room contains an assortment of POW-DERED CREATURES which the Reaver keeps in storage for the odd occasions which crop up in his hectic life. He refined his Particle Blender (see Room 5) to reduce various creatures to a concentrated, powdered form. All they require is added water, and they revert to their original shape. Of course, if only some of the powder is used, the creature will not revert to full size. This is what has happened to the creature currently observing the adventurers. It is a SILVER DRAGON, or rather, a miniature Silver Dragon.

MINIATURE SKILL 6 STAMINA 8 ATTACKS 4
SILVER
DRAGON

Every three Attack Rounds, the Dragon can breathe a sheet of cold at one opponent. The target must roll less than his SKILL on two dice, otherwise he will lose a STAMINA point.

The Dragon will attack as soon as all the adventurers enter the room. It is not entirely aware of its miniaturization, and thinks itself easily a match for a few puny humans.

Most of the powdered creatures are quite mundane. There are plenty of cats, dogs, rabbits and birds, but very few monsters. The Silver Dragon was the pride of the Reaver's collection. The list below gives the selection of monsters which the adventurers may be interested in. If they take some of the animal tubes, you should decide for yourself which creatures they contain. If the adventurers use only a portion of any of the powders, the resulting creature will be small and you should reduce the SKILL and STAMINA scores as you see fit.

	SKILL	STAMINA	ATTACKS
3 CROCODILES	7	7	2
1 DEATH DOG	9	10	1
2 GARKS	7	11	1
1 MAMMOTH	10	16	2
1 MANTICORE	12	18	3
3 NANDIBEARS	9	11	2
1 GIANT SCORPION	10	10	2
4 SLYKK	6	5	1
1 WYRM	9	12	3
2 XOROA	10	11	1

There is a loud gurgling noise coming from the room.
Inside, the large chamber is dominated by three huge vats.
A pulley apparatus hangs from the ceiling above them.
Dangling from this are three repulsive objects. Furthest
away from you is a bleached human skeleton. The two
which are closer have been coated with a jelly. The three are
slowly being pulled along until each is over one of the vats.
They are then lowered. Beyond the vats, eight of the
jelly-like creatures you have encountered before are stand-
ing by a lever, sifting through a pile of bones. As they spot
you, they move towards you menacingly.

The adventurers have discovered the secret of the
Replicanths. The Riddling Reaver has developed a
process for coating skeletons in a jelly-like substance which makes them easy to animate. The resulting creature has a crude intelligence, and may be set
simple tasks and left to get on with them. The
Reaver has set a number of his Replicanths the task
of manufacturing yet more. The process is quite
simple. First a skeleton is assembled from bones
stored in Room 4, with a sticky paste being used to
fuse the bones together. Then the skeleton is hung
from a hook connected to the pulley apparatus.
When the machinery is operated (by the lever), the
skeleton will be moved slowly along the line and
dipped into each of the three vats in turn, until the
Replicanth is finished.

Replicanths are currently being produced at the
rate of one every five minutes. You should keep
track of the time after the adventurers first enter the

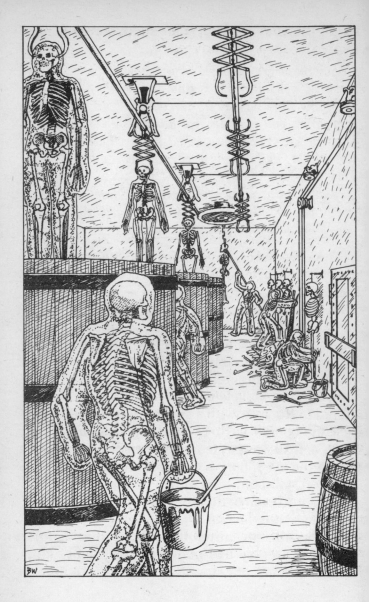

room. If they do not stop the production-line, new Replicanths will be produced.

To stop the production-line, the lever at the far end of the room must be pulled back. But there are eight Replicanths in the way! Each has the following attributes:

REPLICANTH   SKILL 6   STAMINA 4

If the fight lasts more than five minutes, of course, another Replicanth will come off the production-line and join in.

There is a barred iron door halfway down the right-hand wall of this room. The bar can easily be removed, and the door swung open, leading to Room 4.

4

The room is dark, lit only by a faint blue glow from the ceiling. It is full of bones. All the bones that you can see are human bones, although these vary in size. Some are obviously the bones of Pygmies, while others are strangely malformed.

The room is simply a store-chamber for the bones used in the production of the Replicanths. Apart from the iron door, the only other exit is up the steep, narrow chute to the hall above (Scene One, Location 3).

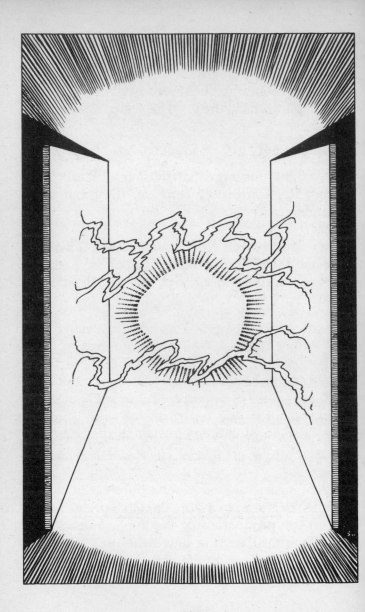

5

This room is quite small, and the light within pulses gently. On its far side stand two plates of metal, two metres square, facing each other. Coloured light dances between them, and high-pitched squeaks hurt your ears.

The Riddling Reaver is well versed in the magical arts, and is also adept at creating and adapting machinery to suit his needs. In this room, he has combined the two. Between the metal plates a magical field has been set up. The field has no effect upon non-living materials. If a living creature passes into it, however, it will start to mutate. Its skin will change colour, its limbs will be warped and twisted, and its hair will fall out. After a few seconds within the field, a creature will lose 1 point of STAMINA, but will gain a peculiar mutation (roll on the Mutant Lizard Man Table, pages 127–9).

The Reaver used this device to create the mutant Lizard Men who serve him out in the jungle.

The room is bare apart from the metal plates, as the presence of too much matter would interfere with the field generated between the plates.

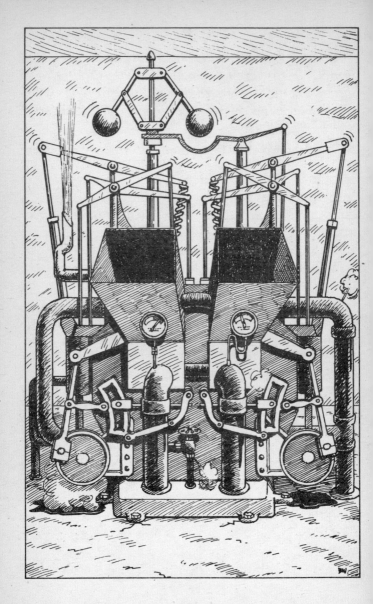

6

The room is dominated by a large black piece of machinery. Steam hisses out of its joints, oil drips on to the floor, and there is grating of metal. It feels as if the machine is a living creature. You can see that there are two chutes built into it on the side facing you.

The machine is a Particle Blender. It was devised many years ago by a wise scholar, who came upon the principle by chance. The machine takes items, separates them into their component particles, and then reassembles them.

If an item is dropped into one of the chutes, there will be a loud whirring and grating, and after a few seconds the item will fall out of a hole round the back of the machine. If examined, it will be found to be undamaged, and slightly cleaner than it was when dropped in. If two items are dropped into the chutes at the same time, though, they will be blended together. What will emerge from the hole at the back will be an item combining the characteristics of the two items. For example, if the adventurers dropped a sword and a shield into the machine, what emerged would be a shield with a sword-blade protruding from it. It is up to you to decide exactly how the characteristics of any items the adventurers drop down the chutes are blended.

The chutes are quite narrow, so an adventurer would have to be very thin to pass down them. They would be unwise to do so, as the process is invariably fatal.

There is nothing else of interest in the room.

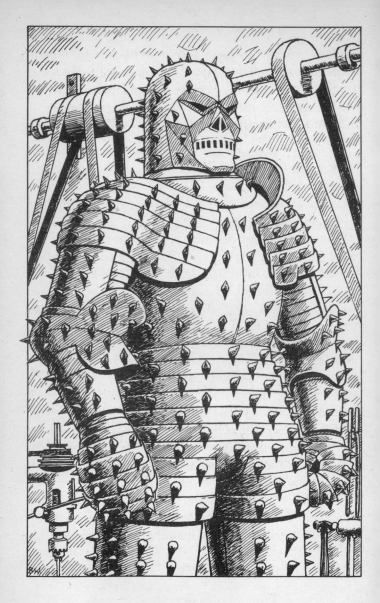

7

This is clearly a work-room of some kind. It is filled with benches, stools and odd-shaped pieces of machinery. In one corner there is a small forge with an anvil, while assorted tools are hanging from the walls. Near by a huge set of plate armour stands proudly. Nearly three metres tall, it is covered with spikes. It is obviously the work of a master armourer, with no area vulnerable to attack.

Most of the pieces of machinery are rejects from failed projects, or scraps which the Reaver felt might come in handy some day. The adventurers may examine them at their leisure, but they will be unable to get them to do anything.

The suit of armour is a different matter. The Riddling Reaver has always been a little sensitive about his fighting prowess. His incredible luck (which derives from his patron gods) makes up for this, but it still irritates him. He therefore built a suit of armour which would make him invincible. Not only would the suit protect him from injury, it would even fight his battles for him! All he would

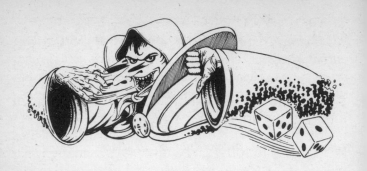

have to do, to be the most feared warrior in Allansia, would be to climb inside and operate the controls. Unfortunately for him, it did not quite work. He could not seem to get the controls to work properly, and the armour had a bad habit of going berserk during tests and wrecking his laboratory. Eventually a new project claimed his attention, and he forgot about his desires to become a mighty warrior.

An adventurer examining the suit of armour will discover that there is a hatch round the back. This will open easily, and one character will be able to ease inside, and into a small control chamber. He will have room to move his arms, and will see a few levers in front of him. One of these is noticeably larger than the others. If the adventurer pulls this lever, the armour will shudder and take a step forward. If the adventurer pulls the same lever again, the armour will step back and slump inert. If he touches any of the other levers, however, the armour will go berserk. It will attack anyone else who is in the room.

226

MECHANICAL ARMOUR
SKILL 14   STAMINA 20

All weapons do −1 damage to the Mechanical Armour. Once the armour's STAMINA is reduced to 5 points, further successful attacks will do 1 point of injury to the adventurer who is inside! The player inside may seek to control the armour when it goes berserk. Pulling the large lever is not enough. He will have to experiment with combinations of levers until the armour is finally deactivated. Every Attack Round the player should roll against SKILL on two dice, adding 4 to the roll. If the result is less than his SKILL, he has succeeded in switching the armour off.

8

Above the door to this room are four brass rings. One still has a piece of frayed rope knotted on to it. When you open the door, you can see nothing inside but blackness. It is not just darkness, but the complete absence of any light at all.

This is the Void Room. It is where the Riddling Reaver disposes of his more troublesome enemies. There is nothing beyond the door but Void. Anyone who steps in, without retaining some contact with the corridor (for example, by having a rope tied around them, held by friends outside the room or tied to the brass rings), will be lost for ever in a Nothingness that exists outside of existence. They may chance to bump into some of the other eternal prisoners of the Void, but this is unlikely, as the Void is infinitely large. Since it is outside existence, there is no way a character lost in the Void can be brought back – even gods are powerless to intervene.

230

9

The large iron door to this chamber has a small grille. As you approach the door you can hear the slow, steady chant of mussed voices coming from it. Looking through the grille, you see a vast rough-carved cavern. The guttering light of over a hundred swaying torches illuminates the cavern. Each is held by a foul jelly-like creature, staring intently at the far end of the cavern. The torches sway in time to the chant, which in turn follows the pounding from the podium at the far end.

There you can see the Riddling Reaver, conducting some bizarre ritual. Behind him, flames shoot up from a lava flow. In front of him lies a tranquil pool of clear water. On either side of him, huge fluted pillars glow with demonic light.

Floating above the pool of water you can see the Pendulum of Fate. The terrific pounding is coming from this. You sense that the artefact is straining against forces which seek to destroy it. The Reaver gesticulates wildly at it, and the pounding gets louder. Your hearts seem to be hammering against your rib-cages in time to the thumping.

The adventurers have arrived in time for the culmination of the Reaver's plan. The ritual is directed at destroying the Pendulum, so that the established order of Good and Evil will be thrown into disarray.

The adventurers will find it very easy to slip into the chamber unobserved, and they will not be spotted until they draw attention to themselves by taking action, or until after five minutes (if the production-line of Room 3 is still working), when a new Replicanth will join its brethren.

There are 132 Replicanths in the chamber, so the adventurers will have to come up with a better plan than charging into battle, if they are to thwart the dastardly plot. Several possibilities exist. Players may think of some ingenious plan that will interrupt the ritual successfully; if they try something that is not covered below, you should use your judgement to decide whether it works. Try to make sure that whatever happens is as dramatic and exciting as possible: remember, this is the climax of the adventure. Think of it like an adventure movie. There should be lots of explosions, plenty of fighting, and success should only just be achieved.

The most obvious ways of putting a stop to the Reaver's machinations involve throwing things over the crowd of Replicanths. A Powdered Creature, thrown into the pool of water in front of the Reaver, would come to life and attack him by surprise. A Yokka Egg thrown successfully would distract him. If the Dice of Logaan were to be thrown they would cause a mighty eruption, as the power of the Trickster Gods of Luck and Chance themselves was turned against their servant.

You should use your judgement in playing out the final scene. There will be plenty of Replicanths to fight, though the confusion will be such that very few of them will be organized enough to spot the adventurers and attack them. It is very important that the heroes keep the Riddling Reaver distracted – and keep confusion reigning. He is such a deadly enemy that if he is allowed time to assess the situation and take organized action, he will be able to defeat the adventurers very rapidly. Once captured, they would not have very much of a chance! No statistics have been given for the Riddling Reaver. He is not an enemy who can be fought in the normal way. Rather you should use your dramatic flair and judgement as GamesMaster to decide the outcome.

Since this is the climactic battle, you should feel free to bend the rules a little to make things work. You should also try to make sure that the Riddling Reaver either escapes destruction at the last moment (getting away in his airship, perhaps), or dies in such a way that his body cannot be recovered (falling into the lava stream would be ideal – with a last manic laugh, of course!). This way you will have set yourself up for the reappearance of the Reaver in a subsequent adventure (after all, it could have been a stuffed Reaver that died, while the real Reaver could have made his getaway). It is astonishing just how enthusiastic players will get about tracking down an old enemy who has eluded them in the past. It is also strange how old enemies seem to have a habit of cheating death!

Ending the Story

You should decide to end the story at the most appropriate moment. It would make sense to end the adventure immediately after the heroes defeat the villain. Making their way back through the

Reaver's Roost would probably be an anticlimax after they have beaten him. Then again, a bit of mopping up of last pockets of resistance would make sense, and the adventurers face the dismal prospect of a trek through the jungle back to civilization.

If you have played through the whole book, you players should now have a saga they can relate with pride. You can now develop your own stories from here, using parts of the plot to help you. The adventurers may return to Kallamehr with the news of their victory. Who knows what thrilling adventure they will find when they get there? That is for you to decide . . . guided, no doubt, by Luck and Chance!

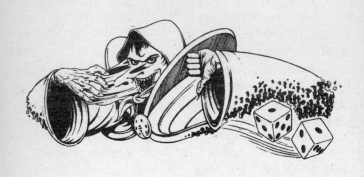

Steve Jackson's
SORCERY!

1. THE SHAMUTANTI HILLS

Your search for the legendary Crown of Kings takes you to the Shamutanti Hills. Alive with evil creatures, lawless wanderers and bloodthirsty monsters, the land is riddled with traps and tricks waiting for the unwary traveller. Will you be able to cross the hills safely and proceed to the second part of the adventure – or will you perish in the attempt?

2. KHARÉ – CITYPORT OF TRAPS

As a warrior relying on force of arms, or a wizard trained in magic, you must brave the terror of a city built to trap the unwary. You will need all your wits about you to survive the unimaginable horrors ahead and to make sense of the clues which may lead to your success – or to your doom!

3. THE SEVEN SERPENTS

Seven deadly and magical serpents speed ahead of you to warn the evil Archmage of your coming. Will you be able to catch them before they get there?

4. THE CROWN OF KINGS

At the end of your long trek, you face the unknown terrors of the Mampang Fortress. Hidden inside the keep is the Crown of Kings – the ultimate goal of the *Sorcery!* epic. But beware! For if you have not defeated the Seven Serpents, your arrival has been anticipated . . .

Complete with all the magical spells you will need, each book can be played either on its own or as part of the whole epic.

Penguin Fantasy Titles
For older readers

THE DRAGONLANCE CHRONICLES

From the creators of DUNGEONS AND DRAGONS now comes DRAGONLANCE, an exciting new fantasy trilogy about the creatures of legend who threaten the destruction of the world of Krynn.

A group of long-time friends – knight and barbarian, warrior and half-elf, dwarf and kender and dark-souled mage – are given the power to save the world. Join their exciting adventures in a quest to find the True Gods and save Krynn from endless night.

1. DRAGONS OF AUTUMN TWILIGHT

A small band of unlikely heroes set out on their quest to save Krynn from the dragons' evil grasp. They have hope – a blue crystal staff in the hands of a beautiful woman – and they have courage. But the forces of evil are strong . . .

2. DRAGONS OF WINTER NIGHT

The darkness deepens and the companions begin a dangerous search for the Dragon Orbs and the legendary Dragonlance, ancient weapons of the True Gods.

3. DRAGONS OF SPRING DAWNING

The dread enemy, Takhisis, the Queen of Darkness, poisons all with her evil. Only Tanis, the leader of the band of heroes has the will to destroy it. He must summon all his strength, courage and faith for the ordeal which lies ahead . . .

THE CRETAN CHRONICLES

John Butterfield, David Honigmann and Philip Parker

1. **BLOODFEUD OF ALTHEUS**
2. **AT THE COURT OF KING MINOS**
3. **RETURN OF THE WANDERER**

Set in the mythological world of Ancient Greece, this 3-book epic brings an exciting historical dimension to Adventure Gamebooks. YOU are Altheus, sent to avenge the death of Theseus, your elder brother, whose body lies trapped in the labyrinth of King Minos. The combat system has been extended to incorporate the concepts of honour and shame.

MAELSTROM

Alexander Scott

Complete with beginners' and advanced rules, referee's notes, maps and charts. *Maelstrom* is a full role-playing game for several players. YOU choose the characters, YOU decide the missions and YOU have the adventures in the turbulent world of Europe in the sixteenth century.

Fantasy Questbooks – 32 pages, full colour

THE PATH OF PERIL
David Fickling and Perry Hinton
Illustrated by Rachel Birkett

The famous explorer, Edmund Mallory, has been foully murdered, and the legendary Bloodstone, which he acquired under mysterious circumstances on his last travels, is missing. All that remains are the scattered fragments of the explorer's diary, his personal notebook and most of the contents of his ransacked study. An almost unsolvable mystery. Yet it seems that the explorer himself expected to meet a violent end and prepared the way for YOU to track down his murderer and recover the Bloodstone. Unfortunately the clues he laid have been scattered in the turmoil of his terrible death. All the information you need is here, ingeniously hidden in both text and pictures, and each strand of the mystery unravels to reveal the next. Are YOU sharp enough to crack it?

STARFLIGHT ZERO
David Fickling and Perry Hinton
Illustrated by Peter Andrew Jones

One by one the Free Planets have fallen to the relentless advance of the Dark Ships until only Caldoran and Palonar remain. Then a last, despairing message comes from Palonar and Caldoran is on its own. It seems that the invaders, armed with the power of the invincible Black Light, will soon conquer the last outpost of resistance. The only hope for the survival of Caldoran is one last desperate mission by a small group of star fighters to strike at the source of the Black Light. And YOU are part of the mission.

HELMQUEST

David Fickling and Perry Hinton

Illustrated by Nik Spender

Atlantis was once a land of peace and prosperity, its golden age assured by the power that Daimos, master of the gods, had invested in the Bright Helm – power to protect the land from evil and sorcery. But then the Helm was shattered into twelve pieces by the dark gods and their servant Vorash. Now each piece lies hidden in a dark and accursed place, protected by one of the evil gods. But YOU have chanced upon the log kept by Na-Manon, priest of Atlantis. This log will reveal the journey made by the evil ones as they concealed each piece of the Helm. Do YOU have it in your power to recover those pieces and remake the Helm, thus restoring peace to Atlantis? All the information you need is there, ingeniously hidden in both text and pictures, and each strand of the mystery unravels to reveal the next. The quest of the Helm awaits you. Do YOU dare to take up the challenge?

THE TASKS OF TANTALON

Steve Jackson

Illustrated by Steven Lavis

Gallantaria is reeling from the aftermath of a long and costly war. Tantalon, wizard of the court, rules the kingdom over an Inner Council of scheming knights, jealously vying for power. But Tantalon's years are drawing to a close. In order to seek out the kingdom's sharpest minds, Tantalon has devised an epic adventure quest. YOU are a competitor in the Sorcerer's quest: can YOU steal the Brimstone Dragon's treasure hoard? Will YOU find a way to free Sir Dunstable from imprisonment in the Stinn dungeon? And how will YOU catch the Demon Fish? All the information you need is ingeniously woven into the text and pictures. All YOU have to do is to take up the challenge and crack the mystery!